with your friends.

with your friends.

William Grant

William Grant Publishing

William Grant Publishing
with your friends.
Copyright © 2022 William Grant
All Rights Reserved.
Cover Design by Amber Burnett
ISBN: 978-0-578-39017-8

CONTENTS

1   1

2   7

3   11

4   15

5   17

6   24

7   35

8   39

9   46

10   54

11   62

12   76

13   81

CONTENTS

14   84

15   93

16   97

17   101

18   104

19   112

20   115

21   123

22   128

23   131

24   134

25   139

26   151

27   158

28   160

29   167

30   171

CONTENTS

31	175
32	193
33	196
34	199
35	201
36	208
37	212

| ACKNOWLEDGEMENTS | 217 |
| AUTHOR BIO | 219 |

For Mema and Granddaddy,
who taught me how to have faith.

Is this what love is?

The screaming got louder.

"I'm so sick of getting interrogated every time I come home. I thought marriage was supposed to be about trust." My father's deep voice thundered through the floor.

"Is it wrong for me to wonder what you're doing at work that keeps you out so late? Is that really too much?" It was quieter, but there was the tear-filled pleading of my mother.

"I'm WORKING, Melanie. I'm putting food on the table for you and our son. Can't you be a little more *grateful*?!"

I heard a thud and my hands twisted around the flashlight in my hand as I knelt on the floor of my closet. The pillow against my back slid further down the wall as I leaned forward and pushed the blanket from my lap. There was silence for what felt like minutes.

My mother. "Don't throw things, Saul. Peter might wake up. Do you want him to hear this?" The last words were sharp with anger.

No words came after that. I held my breath as I waited for what would come next. Were they really done? My answer came in the sound of the creak from the floorboards beneath my mother's feet as she passed the door to my room. The silence I'd been waiting for all night finally came, the real silence. Turning back to the wall of my closet, I shined the green flashlight across the words once more.

"Talk to me, Brooke," I whispered in the dark. My eyes moved along the wall, searching for a response.

Where'd my friends go?

"I'm your friend. You're the only one I've got. Is that okay?" I looked for a response, but there was nothing new for her to say anymore.

Before we moved in, our house had been owned by another family. I didn't know much about them except that they had a daughter named Brooke and she had my room, or that's what I assumed from the wall. Scrawled in different places along the side wall in the closet were messages, quotes from the room's previous occupant. They were written in sharpie, over a dozen, spread out across the bottom of the wall. They were like inner thoughts that were too private to share:

I don't know how to do this.

Who am I becoming?

The only reason I thought the author's name was Brooke was because one of them actually had a name:

Get it together, Brooke.

There was something nice about it, the anonymity of it. Most nights were spent here, alone and talking to the only friend I had.

My legs were almost asleep from lack of movement when I finally stood up and stepped out of my closet. The dim moonlight shone through my window, casting dark shadows across the hardwood floor. I could hear the soft pat of raindrops outside. The clock on my bedside table showed 1:17 a.m. I walked around my bed to the window. My freckled face appeared in the glass, looking back at me as I gazed out at the dark street. My father called our neighborhood "The Grid," everything perfectly built to fit within the perfect lines of our perfect streets. All the houses were dark except the one directly across from ours, another two-story brick box. There was a dim light in one of the windows. Who was it? What were they doing? Were they happy? Were they lonely, too?

I turned and walked back around my bed, over to my desk with my schoolbooks and unfinished novel strewn across it. Even in the dark, the half-finished sentence was visible on the page of my notebook. The yelling had started, and I'd crawled into my closet, leaving Connor holding out his empty hand and wondering if he'd ever find a place in his world where he could feel safe. The answer still hung somewhere in the empty space.

I paused at my door, listening to the quiet outside. Opening the door, I stepped into the bathroom across the hall. I shut the door before turning on the light. Sitting on the toilet lid, I closed my eyes and wrapped my arms around my stomach. I tried clearing my head from the echoes of my parents' fight, focusing on the things around me instead. The tiled floor felt cold against my bare feet. The air conditioning ruffled my hair as it blew from the vent above me. I took a few deep breaths and opened my eyes. There was a tightness in my chest that I knew wouldn't go away, but my head was clear enough that maybe sleep would come now. I stood up and walked over to the sink, splashing some water onto my face. The slight stubble on my cheeks prickled against my fingers as I scratched at my jaw, moving my hand up to run through my messy auburn hair. Drying my hands on the towel by the sink, I turned out the light and opened the door. When I turned to walk back to my room, I heard a noise. There was snoring coming from downstairs. I crept to the top of the stairs and listened for a moment. The snoring got louder before going silent again. I turned and walked back to my room and got in the bed. My father was spending another night on the couch.

Drops of rain slid off the roof in front of the kitchen window as I looked out to see the sun stretching over our bright green lawn. I loved the way the world looked after it rained. Everything was brighter, colors more vibrant. It relieved the lingering tension of last night.

My mom came into the kitchen dressed in her navy-blue nursing scrubs. Her bright red hair was pulled back into a ponytail, loose strands hanging around her head. Her eyes were distant as she moved to the counter, absentmindedly picking up a plate from the sink and beginning to wash it as I sat down at the table.

"Sleep all right?" she asked, gazing out the window as she scrubbed the plate lazily. Her question sounded half-empty, like she wasn't listening for an answer.

I didn't want to tell her that I didn't go to sleep till around four because I was listening to her cry, just like I'd heard her all the other nights.

"It was okay," I replied.

She placed the plate on the drying rack and moved on to the next, seemingly unaware of my omission, "I thought I heard you get up. I had trouble sleeping myself."

"I'm sorry," I said.

Her scrubbing picked up slightly, her pressure on the plate becoming more aggressive. There was a tension in her arms as her hand slid back and forth across the plate, suds building around her fingers.

"Mom."

"It's not your fault." She stopped scrubbing, moving the plate beneath the water and holding it there. The water slid across the blue surface and over her knuckles. There was an almost undetectable sigh as she placed the dish into the drying rack.

Turning off the water, she reached into a drawer by the sink and pulled out a knife. She picked up our last two bananas, peeled one, and began to cut it up. I watched as she sliced it into thin slivers before placing them on a paper towel. After cutting up the first banana, she stepped to the fridge and made a mark on the erasable calendar that kept track of her daily weight checks. Mom had been on a diet for two months. She'd been keeping tabs on her weight over the past couple months, watching it fluctuate up and down, never getting to where she wanted to be. Her shoulders slumped as she walked back to the counter and picked up a knife, peeling a banana and cutting it into small slivers.

I sat up straighter in my chair as I heard my father's footsteps coming down the stairs. Mom stopped peeling a second banana for just a moment, eyes trained on her hands. She resumed her work as he stepped into the room.

Like every morning, he had on his Berghoff Elevators uniform as he entered the room, black hair combed flat across the top of his head. I watched his shoulders hunch forward as he sat down at the table and bent down to tie his shoes. His jaw was tight, and his eyes didn't leave his shoelaces. Mom stopped what she was doing and turned to him. Her eyes looked in his direction but didn't quite land on him. She watched him for a moment before speaking.

"Will you be home for dinner?" Her hands gripped the edge of the countertop like she was bracing herself for something.

Silence. This was how he was when they had a fight, quiet and unforgiving.

"Will you be home for dinner?" she spoke louder this time. He had to have heard her, but she would never call him on it.

Still more silence. I watched him as he tied his shoelaces, pulling them tight and roping them together with an unwavering attention to the movement of his hands. He wasn't going to give in to her. I hated when he was like this. Watching these interactions, watching him be so cold to her, just felt exhausting. I wasn't in their fight, but, as an only child, I felt a part of it anyway.

"Please just answer me, Saul." I could see her hands gripping the edge of the counter as she looked at him, hope in her eyes. I wanted to be next to her, holding her hand, giving her some kind of strength or comfort.

He had his shoes on by then and got up to leave, "No." He slammed the door, not looking in her direction for even a second.

She stood there, staring at the door as if she were waiting for him to come back; waiting for him to open the door, kiss her on the cheek, tell her he'd be home and couldn't wait to have dinner with her. I could see her body settle as she accepted he wasn't coming back. Her shoulders slipped, the lines around her mouth curving, eyes going back down to the counter. She closed her eyes for a moment, breathing slowly. Finally, she opened her eyes and turned back to the counter. She picked up the knife and began cutting up the remainder of the banana.

I tried to think of something, anything I could say or do that would help her. Nothing. I was useless.

In a year I'd be going to college and the thought of leaving her here like this, hurting and filled with so much sadness felt cruel. What kind of son would do that?

I stood up, threw the remainder of my apple in the trash and walked over to the sink to wash my hands. She was silent as I rinsed my hands clean and dried them on a paper towel. I stood there for a moment next to her, hoping that just being there would bring her comfort. I brought my hand up to her back and rubbed gently. She stopped cutting for a moment, just a moment, and looked out the window. I followed the line of her eyes to a bird as it hopped across the yard, picking at various spots in the grass. When it finally flew away, her eyes went back down to her hands. She began cutting again. I stood for just a moment longer, before heading up the stairs to get my school bag, the soft tap of the knife echoing my footsteps.

2

The parking lot of East Haverty High was flooded with kids when I got to school. For some reason, people at my school liked to hang out there. Apparently, there were too many couches in the student lounge or something. I wound my way through the congestion of cars and students, bypassing groups of juniors and seniors talking and texting and taking selfies with each other.

When I reached the doorway to my first class, I found Mrs. Stroud bent over a desk, trying to slide it to the back of the room. Her dark skin was silhouetted by the harsh sunlight shining through the windows. I could see the sharp angles of her chin as it jutted out in her efforts. Setting my bag by the door, I moved to the other side of the desk and began to pull.

"Thank you!" she exclaimed with a heavy breath as the desk began to move across the floor, "These heavy-ass desks!"

I gave a little laugh as we got the desk into place. Mrs. Stroud stood up, her beaded necklace rattling against her chest. The red sweater she was wearing looked almost pink in the light.

"I don't understand why those sonsabitches can't move the desks back themselves. I mean it's a class full o' big honkin' men!" She shook her head as I laughed at her swearing, which she rarely did in front of other students.

She was referring to the night school class that met on Wednesday nights. It was an Algebra class for the GED program. Apparently, most of the participants in the class were well-muscled, middle-aged men.

Most of them, in fact, worked with my father. It was a common occurrence to come in on a Thursday morning and find the chairs scattered across the room for reasons unknown.

"Have you talked to Principal Hughes about it?" I asked, straightening up one of the desks. "I'm sure he could say something to them."

She wiped her hands on her jeans, "Nope, I will not allow him to take care of my problems for me. I'll leave them *another* polite note and see what happens." Walking to the other side of her desk, she picked up her Teacher of the Year tote bag and began taking out her folders. "Now, do you have any pages for me?"

I'd known Mrs. Stroud since I was little. She was my Sunday School teacher from kindergarten to fifth grade and, since starting high school, I'd had three classes with her. When she first started, she'd applied for the 20th Century Literature position, but was beat out by Mr. Jameson. The History spot was the only other one available. She'd bounced around over the past few years, teaching European History, Art History, and Russian History. I'd had her for European and Art the past two years.

"I reworked parts of Chapter 12. I think it flows better now." I handed her sixteen pages out of my bag.

She flipped through them, "Good, I'll look over them at lunch. Have you taken another crack at the ending?"

I sighed, "I'm still working on it. I think I just need to take some more time with it."

"Don't rush through it. You've made some real progress over the last year. Don't force it just because you want this first draft done. You'll never get anything good by forcing it out of you. Just remember, you don't have to wrap everything up in a bow. Part of why your writing, and this story, is so good is because it feels real. The relationship between Amber and Connor feels authentic because they see each other's pain. It's honest. Keep that going all the way through to the end."

"I'll try," I said, nodding.

As other students began to enter the room, I took my seat in the second row. I watched as Mrs. Stroud straightened things on her desk before standing up. Her back straightened as she stood, shoulders moving back. For the better part of our conversation she'd been relaxed, sitting in a comfortable slouch. Now she held herself high, stepping into her teacher skin.

When Mrs. Stroud first began teaching at East Haverty, some of the parents had some complaints about her teaching style. She would swear occasionally, making references to movies and shows that parents deemed "inappropriate" for high schoolers. After a talk with Principal Hughes, she began teaching in a more formal way. She never swore and made references only to movies that were PG-13 or lower.

She still talked the same around me though. She told me that, as a writer, I shouldn't censor myself. I think she meant it more along the lines of the topics I chose, but I knew it was also a reason for her to let down her guard for a few minutes during the day.

"All right," she began, turning to look at the class as the last few stragglers wandered in and sat down. "Who can summarize last night's reading for those who didn't do it?"

I went home for lunch.

There was an elderly couple, Ira and Adelaide Basset, that lived down the street from our house. Every day, at exactly 11:30 in the morning, they would go for a walk. They'd come out of their house with their hats and canes and walk around the block twice, three times if the weather was nice. This usually took about an hour, at the end of which they would get into their car and, presumably, go to lunch. I would pass them on my way home when I went off campus for lunch. Sometimes they would be walking in silence while at other times they'd be deep in conversation, their paper-thin lips sliding back and forth.

When I pulled in the driveway and got out of my car, they were passing in front of my house. They looked over at me as I walked to my door and gave a little wave, Mr. Basset lifting his cane into the air and shaking it at me with a smile. I waved back, smiling, as I stepped inside and shut the door.

The house was silent as I entered the kitchen and began making a sandwich. There was something nice about being there when no one else was home. The quiet peace was soothing. It was easier to think.

We bought the house two years earlier. My father had gotten a raise at the factory that allowed us to finally upgrade from the two-bedroom condo we'd been in since I was four. We'd been trying to find a place for several years, but nothing fell within our price range. When the raise finally came, my parents expanded their budget and found this place. I knew my parents had wanted it to be a fresh start for us, but it just hadn't worked out that way. You can fight in any house.

I had the sandwich finished off by the time I got upstairs. Pulling my notebook out of my bag, I opened my closet door and sat down on the spread-out blanket that was placed across the bottom beneath my hanging clothes.

I glanced over the wall, jumping from message to message, waiting for Brooke to speak.

Is there more?

I don't know, Brooke, I thought as I turned to the page I'd stopped at the night before, *you tell me.*

3

Mom and I were sitting at the kitchen table over plates of meatloaf, green beans, and mashed potatoes. My father's plate sat in the microwave, covered with a paper towel. My mom had to stay at work an hour longer than normal, so I had gotten dinner together. I had overcooked the meatloaf a bit and the potatoes were a little too salty, but the green beans were perfect. My mom was a great cook. She was one of those people who could throw a bunch of random ingredients into a bowl and it would suddenly be a feast from a Food Network show. A couple times she had tried to teach me, but it had just ended poorly when I tried it on my own.

"These potatoes are great," she said as she scooped up the last two bites from her plate.

I laughed, "No, they're not and you don't have to pretend that they are. I've accepted the fact that I'm going to die alone and hungry." I stood up and took my plate to the sink, "Do you want seconds?"

"Nope! I've gotta stick to small portions. And you're not going to die alone, don't say that." She waved her hand in my direction like she was swatting a fly.

"Ah, but you didn't say I wouldn't be hungry!" I replied.

She laughed. It was nice when she laughed.

"So how was work? Why did you have to stay late?"

She stood up and brought her plate over to the sink. I pulled some containers from the cabinet next to her head to put the leftovers into.

"There was some confusion with someone's chart. The new girl had marked it wrong and one of the night nurses needed someone to clarify a dosage. Overall, it was a good day though. There's this one woman," she gripped the edge of the sink as she leaned forward, laughing to herself. "She's eighty-two years old. I was checking her vitals and she just looked up at me and said, out of the blue and very matter-of-factly, 'Herbert, I will *not* be engaging in intercourse with you this evening.'"

We both busted out laughing. My mom's smile made the room brighter. There were so many times where a smile was impossible for her, the times where things were bad with my father. During those times, she might go a day or two without cracking a smile or laughing. When she did smile, it was like it made up for all the time she spent frowning. She had the kind of smile that just made you happy to be looking at it. After what had happened that morning, I felt a sense of accomplishment at being able to bring it out.

"I shouldn't laugh," she said, trying to calm herself down. "It's really not a funny situation this woman is in, but it was just so unexpected." One of the interesting things about mom working in a hospital was that she usually came home with some pretty strange stories. There was one time when she was helping a male patient get back into his bed and he suddenly vomited into the front collar of her shirt. Mom said she had stayed in the shower for thirty minutes after that.

"It's only bad if you laughed in her face," I replied as I put the last pot in the dishwasher.

"No, no, no. I just said 'Okay' and went to laugh in the hallway."

"Good." I smiled as she dried her hands off on a dish towel. Strands of her hair floated around the sides of her face, loose from her ponytail. It was nice when things were like this: happy and light. It never seemed to stay that way for very long. "All right, I gotta go do homework. Are you going up to bed?"

"I will in a little bit. I'm going to go ahead and make my lunch for tomorrow."

She turned and opened the refrigerator door, taking out a head of lettuce. I stood there for a moment, watching her with her back turned towards me. There was a lightness to her movements as she pulled off leaves of lettuce to use for her salad. As I turned and headed up the stairs, I heard my father coming in the kitchen door.

It happened quickly. Within fifteen minutes of him getting home, they were fighting. It never took long. It wasn't something they worked up to. They would just all of a sudden be in the middle of an argument, no prior threats or anticipation. There were times where I think they did it because they didn't know what else to do. Arguing had become part of their routine.

"But every night?" she would ask each time. "Why do you have to work late almost every single night?"

"Because" my father would respond, his voice beginning to get louder, "I'm trying to put food on our table and a roof over our heads."

He worked late most nights, coming home after dinner was already put away in containers in the refrigerator. It was rare that we would all eat together at the same time, usually only occurring on Sundays which were his day off. Even then, he would sometimes have to go into work to resolve some issue at the factory. We just didn't do that much as a family. He had worked at Berghoff for most of my life and the long hours had been fairly consistent throughout the years. It had been that way particularly during my younger, elementary school years. He would come home and we might all watch a movie on the couch or, occasionally, play a board game. Most days though, he worked late. Our chances of creating that father-son relationship that was so prominent in movies started slowly slipping away until it seemed like we had missed it. By the time I had reached my senior year, it felt like the opportunity was gone. It didn't help things when I heard them arguing. He would use his words as weapons. There were times when he would tell her she was being stupid or call her a bitch. He'd only started saying he hated her in the past year. I couldn't understand how anybody could say that to somebody that they still claimed to love.

"Will you just leave me alone? I don't want to talk about this anymore!" My father would be talking with his hands. He always talked with his hands when he was angry.

"I want to know why you have to work late every night! I don't understand why you would have to work late every *single* night!" Even from the second floor, I could hear the tears in my mother's voice.

"Because maybe I don't want to come home and be verbally assaulted when I walk in the door! Did you ever think about that?" He would be extending his neck forward, eyes locked on hers. I had seen it too many times when I would come home in the middle of the battle.

"Oh, so you'd just rather stay at work than come home to your *family?*"

"If it means coming home to this, than yeah!"

I heard soft footsteps coming down the hallway and then the bathroom door shut. My mother. There was silence for several moments before my father's heavy boots came thumping down the hallway. I could hear him enter their bedroom and sit on the bed. He took his shoes off and went into their bathroom to get a shower. Getting up, I stepped over to my bedroom door and quietly opened it.

Everything was silent except for the soft spray of the shower coming from their closed bathroom door. I slipped into the hallway to the other bathroom, the one my mother had locked herself inside of. Soft sniffles and deep breaths came from the other side of the door. I stood there, listening to my mother's heartache being contained within the small room. I wanted to knock, to ask her to come out, to find the words that could give her the relief she was looking for. But I couldn't do that. My mind could not develop the kind of words that would have that power. I sighed quietly, leaning my head against the door frame. Why couldn't I help her?

I listened to her cry for a few more seconds before stepping back to my room and shutting the door.

The next morning, my father was putting his shoes on in the living room when I got downstairs. I headed into the kitchen and a few minutes later he followed.

"Good morning," he said as he pulled an apple out of our fruit bowl and took a bite, his jet-black hair combed perfectly into place.

"Good morning," I replied. I didn't look at him as I poured some cereal into a bowl.

He picked up the newspaper off the counter and spread it out in front of him. Flipping through, he found the Local News page and leaned forward to read an article, his elbows pressing into the inky paper.

I put the milk back in the refrigerator and took my bowl over to the table and sat down.

"How's school?" My father asked, not looking up from the paper.

"It's school. Nothing special."

"Are your grades okay?"

"I think so." He never looked up at me, eyes staying on the paper, no recognition as to whether he was actually listening to me or not. I felt like I could say I was failing every class and he wouldn't even blink. His eyes didn't even move over the page in front of him, just lingering somewhere in the middle.

He stood up straight. "Good. I've got to go to work." Folding the paper up, he dropped it back down on the counter with a snap. He walked over to the table and picked up his jacket, sliding his arms through the sleeves, not bothering to zip it up as he opened the door to the driveway.

"See you later," he called, not waiting to hear my response before shutting the door behind him.

I sat there in the silence, listening as I heard his car door open, then close, then the sound of the ignition turning over. There was a soft rumble as he backed out of the driveway.

"See ya."

I spent Saturday morning working on my writing. Mrs. Stroud had told me to start working on the climax of the story and it was proving more difficult than I had originally thought. Everything I was putting down felt contrived and fake. The words that my characters were saying didn't sound real. It was all just crap. Not to mention the fact that I couldn't figure out how to get Amber and Connor back together by the end. I finally gave up and decided to go for a drive.

After driving aimlessly for a while, I pulled into the parking lot of the Empty Cup. I hadn't discovered a love for coffee yet, but I didn't want to go home.

I opened the glass-paned door of the Empty Cup and stepped inside, the *whoosh* of passing cars going silent as it closed behind me with a gentle click. The soft murmur of conversation and the hiss of steaming milk filled my ears. Tables were being occupied by different kinds of people, hipsters with their bushy beards and black-rimmed glasses, a few old ladies with their warm sweaters and fragile hands. It wasn't too crowded; eight of the fifteen tables being taken. The air was thick with the scent of coffee beans and croissants. I looked around at the walls, two of which were covered with floor-to-ceiling bookshelves filled with books and their small comforts. Soft, coffee flavored whispers flitted through the air, filling the space with a welcoming intimacy. Heads were leaned down over steamy mugs of hot chocolate and lattes.

When I approached the counter, I found Theresa Dredson, from my school, standing behind it, book in hand and a grimace on her face.

Her long black hair was pulled into a ponytail which only made her expression harsher. She looked up at me, rolled her eyes, and tossed the book onto the counter behind her.

"What can I get you?" she asked, her voice sounding anything but helpful.

I glanced over the menu, "Um, I think I'll just take a water."

This elicited a scoff and another eye roll, "Seriously? You came to a coffeehouse to get some water?"

"Yeah, I guess so."

HA!" she turned around, picking up a cup and walking to the sink. Holding the cup under the faucet, she glared at me as the cup filled with water. Fixing a top on it, she plopped it down in front of me and tossed a straw in my direction which landed on the floor. "There, now go sit in the corner with the children's books. Enjoy your waaaater." She drew the last word out in the mocking tone of a toddler taunting a classmate.

I picked up the water and grabbed a table by a window in an empty corner of the room. Reaching up to the shelf behind me, I pulled down a book. *Of Mice and Men*. I opened it up but didn't start reading. Instead, I peered over the top at the other patrons. An elderly woman sat at a table, a big scrapbook covering the top. She moved several pictures around searching for the right arrangement. Her pursed lips got tighter and tighter as she slid the pictures around the page. Finding the right spot, she pulled out a glue stick and spread thick purple stripes across the back of each one. As she pressed the pictures down with manicured fingernails, her lips loosened, and a satisfied smile spread across her face.

Diving into my book, I slipped away from the world around me. I was half-way through the book when a voice reached my ears.

"I think you've been stood up."

Looking up, I found that the table to my left had become occupied. Two guys and a girl, all looking about my age, were watching me. "What do you mean?"

"Well, you've been sitting there since before we got here which was thirty minutes ago." said the guy who had first spoken. He had curly, black hair that hung down across his forehead. His eyes were green and filled with what seemed to be a genuine curiosity as they stared into mine.

"Oh, no, I'm not actually waiting on anyone."

The girl smiled at me as she pushed a strand of dark brown hair behind her ear, "Well, being alone is fine, but you're welcome to come sit with us. No pressure though." A smile spread across her face as she gestured to the empty fourth side of their square table.

I closed my book, "I think I'm gonna go. I don't want to intrude on you guys. I mean, you don't even know me. Thanks though." As I got up to leave, the boy pushed me back down with a hand on my shoulder. He reached his other hand down between my legs to the edge of my chair and pulled it across the gap between our tables.

"Come on, just for a little bit. I'm sure you're not a serial killer," he replied, settling back in his chair. "I'm Kevin."

"Mallory," chimed in the girl.

"I'm Ryan." The boy directly across from me lifted a hand from his iced coffee to give a little wave. His dark blonde hair was cut short and neat. He had blue eyes that never quite met mine. There was a sadness in his features, from his slumped shoulders to the nervous smile that didn't make it up to his eyes. It was clear that there was some kind of weight on his back, something holding him down. He seemed slightly unsure about the new addition to their group. He looked down at his coffee as he swirled it slowly, watching the black liquid slip around the melting ice cubes. There was something sweetly beautiful about him, something I couldn't quite figure out.

"So, what's your bio?" Mallory asked. "Name, heritage, social security number, etc."

I smiled, "Uh, my name's Peter, I might be German, and my social security number is classified information."

They laughed, "Well, I like you already!" Kevin exclaimed. "I'm guessing you go to East Haverty? You don't look like a familiar character from our little west side story."

"Yeah, I'm East."

"Nice. So were you just hanging out here reading or...?"

"I didn't really have anything else to do so I was just killing time before going back to homework."

"Well, if you ask me, you're better off. I mean, who wants to spend a Saturday working on schoolwork when you can hang with the three sexiest homies you'll ever meet?" Mallory said, spreading her arms wide. "Now, let's get you some more coffee."

"It's water, actually." I replied, feeling a little silly. "Tried coffee once, didn't do much for me.

She leaned forward on the table, eyebrows raised, "Oh, friend, we gotta fix that right now."

Mallory got up and walked over to the counter, coming back minutes later with an iced coffee and a vanilla latte. I preferred the latte, but I had to admit that coffee was much better iced than hot.

"All right, now that we've gotten that situation taken care of, we can get to know each other a little better. Let's play twenty questions." she said.

"Seriously?" Kevin replied, "Twenty questions?"

"Yessss. We can get to know each other AND break any ice that might still be floating around."

"Okay, fine. You go first than."

Mallory smiled, "Gladly. So, who's your favorite musical artist?"

"Lenny Kravitz." Kevin shot out, whistling *American Woman.*

I laughed, "Fleetwood Mac."

"Same." Ryan smiled in my direction.

"Adele." said Mallory, taking another sip of her coffee.

"Wait! What? No! You can't bring Adele into this!" Kevin leaned forward across the table, "That's like being asked who your hero is and saying Jesus!"

Mallory came right back at him, a finger in his face, stern expression, "Don't you disrespect the LORD! You know better than that! Sit yourself back down!"

"You know what I mean! Certain levels of perfection aren't allowed in this game."

"Still. Don't you tell me who to like." They stared at each other for a moment, eye to eye, before Kevin slipped back into his chair with a smile on his face. Mallory did the same, rolling her eyes and matching his smile. "Someone else go."

"Any guilty pleasures?" Kevin asked in a deep, dramatic voice. "Mine are gummy bears and *The Amazing Race.*"

Ryan lifted his cup and shook it. Iced Coffee.

"I can pretty much devour an entire bag of chocolate covered pretzels in one sitting," I said, patting my stomach.

"Mmmmm" Kevin hummed, looking from me to Mallory.

She leaned back in her chair and stretched her arms over her head, "I don't have any."

"Oh, really?" Kevin asked, giving her a "you're shittin' me" look.

"Really." She shrugged her shoulders, "I don't feel guilty over things I like."

From the other side of the table, Ryan looked up from his coffee. "Is that why you lied about binging *Gossip Girl* last weekend?" he asked quietly, a smile playing at his lips.

"Boom," Kevin said, slapping his hand down on the table.

Mallory crossed her arms over her chest, "Fine. Whatever."

We kept going like that for an hour. I learned that Mallory loved photography and Kevin played on the West Haverty High soccer team and Ryan's favorite movie was *Cloud Atlas.* It was surprising how easy I fell into the rhythm that they had with each other. They didn't treat me like I was the new guy in the group. It was like I was already one of them, one of their friends.

It was clear early on that Ryan didn't talk much. At first, I just thought it was because of me, that maybe he was shy around strangers.

But when he got up to go to the restroom, I asked Kevin and Mallory about it.

"Don't take it personally. He doesn't talk much in general. He's a pretty quiet guy. Once you get to know him, he'll open up to you a little more." Kevin explained, pushing dark curls out of his eyes as he looked at me.

"Why doesn't he talk much?"

"Ryan's had some trouble in the past, some stuff at his old school. He doesn't like us to mention it." Mallory said, looking back towards the restrooms for Ryan.

I wondered what kind of trouble he'd been in that made him so quiet. Whatever the case, there was something interesting about him that I couldn't quiet figure out. As we sat there, I watched him as he watched us, following our conversation without adding much more than an occasional comment. Every now and then he would get lost somewhere, his eyes going distant for a moment before fluttering back into focus. I wondered where he went during those times.

While Ryan was mostly silent, Kevin and Mallory were the opposite. They kept our conversation up, moving through a variety of topics about me, them, school, and anything else that came up. They had a quick kind of banter with each other that was pretty funny to watch. At one point, Mallory started giving Kevin crap for saying that he thought women peed out of their butts when he was little.

"Dude, *seriously?*" she said, leaning forward over the table to look at him through wide eyes.

He rolled his eyes, "I was a *kiiiid*. I obviously don't think that anymore."

"YA SURE?" Mallory replied. "Do we need to have an anatomy lesson?"

"Oh, do you have a map of the human body in your purse?"

"Of course. You never know when you need to instruct someone on how to find the fallopian tubes." She picked up her phone, glancing at the time. "All right, I gotta get home. Hey, we should exchange numbers so we can hang out with you again. I mean, unless you were having more fun with George and Lennie. Totally understandable."

I laughed. We exchanged numbers and then headed out to the parking lot. Ryan got in the car with Mallory, who was giving him a ride home. Kevin walked over to a beat-up Toyota, getting inside and giving it a couple tries before the engine finally turned over. As I pulled out of the parking lot and headed home, I felt happy. The day had turned out much different than I had expected, but it was okay.

For the first time in a while, I wasn't thinking about my parents or school or college. My mind was focused on something else: the fact that, for the first time in years, I might actually be making friends.

6

The next morning, I woke up to three text messages from Mallory and one from Kevin:

Mallory: *Wanna meet us at the mall this afternoon?*
Mallory: *At 2:30?*
Kevin: *Hey! Has Mallory texted you yet?*
Mallory: *You're probably not awake*

I smiled and quickly replied that I would meet them. Getting out of bed, I began getting ready for church. My parents were in their room and I could see my Mom sitting at her vanity as I walked past their door to get to the bathroom. She was brushing through her long red hair, the strands falling around her shoulders in waves. My father was sitting on the edge of the bed putting on his loafers, his red tie hanging loose around his neck. They were talking about someone at his job. It was nice to see them acting normal for a change, no arguing or yelling. Their voices were calm as they spoke, and I tried to remember the last time I'd heard them talk like that to each other. It had been weeks, at the very least. The last time I could remember was the night before school started. My father had that Sunday off, so we all had dinner at the kitchen table. It was one of those rare occasions where we actually did something together, as a family. We'd sat around the table and talked about my senior year and what my parents had been like when they'd been my age. They'd met in high school, graduated in the same year, and gone on to Northwestern together. When they talked about their time there, they both seemed happy.

I stepped down the hallway and into the restroom. As I put toothpaste on my toothbrush, I listened to their voices coming through the wall. It was a soft murmur, but it was there.

My church wasn't a big cathedral with stain-glass windows and a brass bell. It was a small brick building with large windows that were graying from age. The windows were often shuttered. The sanctuary was painted a soft yellow with hardwood floors that creaked so often they sounded like a back-up to the organ. The old wooden pews were cushioned in deep blue and smelled like they came out of someone's attic. Little crosses were carved into the ends of each pew. The pulpit stood tall at the front left corner of the sanctuary, the alter at the center. A large golden cross stood atop the alter.

"Good morning, Peter."

I looked up from where I was sitting in the pew to find Mrs. Stroud standing over me, smiling. She was wearing a flowing lavender dress with a gold cross hanging on a chain around her neck. Behind her was a young guy, around my age, with buzzed hair, green eyes, and skin the same shade as Mrs. Stroud's. This was her son, Alexander. We had been in the same Sunday School class as kids. He went to West Haverty High, so I didn't know much about who he was now except for what Mrs. Stroud had told me in conversation. He was into filmmaking and made short films in his free time.

"Good morning," I said, smiling back.

"Where are your parents?" she asked, glancing around the sanctuary.

I looked back at the doorway, the two large wooden doors, and into the lobby, "They're out there getting coffee, I think."

When I turned back to look at her, she was watching my face. "You gonna have new pages for me this week?"

"Yeah, they should be ready by tomorrow." I nodded.

"Good, I'll see you in class." She brought her hand down to my shoulder and squeezed it gently before walking away.

Mrs. Stroud knew about my parents, that they weren't happy. She had never said anything to me about them, but somehow, I knew. There was something about the way she watched us, the way she took notice of all the times my father was missing from Sunday services or other events, the cold silence when he was in attendance. I knew she wasn't judging me for it. That wasn't who Mrs. Stroud was. She just watched, knowing.

I got to the mall around two o'clock. I wasn't meeting them until 2:30, but I didn't want to sit around at home doing nothing for forty-five minutes. The parking lot wasn't packed for a Sunday, so I found a parking space without trouble.

Needing to kill some time, I strolled around the mall for a bit. There weren't many people inside, mostly elderly couples and people walking for exercise. At the center of the mall was a large water fountain with several benches collected around it. I sat down at one of them and watched the water cascade down the concrete grooves and walls of the fountain. My left foot tapped rhythmically against the tiled floor. I felt odd, strangely nervous.

I didn't have friends. There were people I knew and people I talked to sometimes, but no one that I would call a real friend. I didn't feel like I *needed* friends. The kids in my school weren't people that I connected with or related to, so it was fine that I wasn't close to them. It did get a little lonely sometimes though.

But now I was making friends. Maybe. I had only hung out with them once, but I already wanted to know them more. There was something exciting about seeing them again. Kevin and Mallory were so fun and friendly, something I had never been. And Ryan, there was something about him. I didn't know what it was, but I was curious.

It was finally reaching 2:30. Mallory had texted me as I was leaving church, telling me to meet them in the food court, so I got up and headed that way. The food court at the Haverty mall was pretty big. The space was a large semi-circle with ten different restaurants to choose from, plus smoothie and cookie kiosks. The walls were a deep red that contrasted the cream-colored floors. In the center of the area was a cluster of guacamole green tables, each with four chairs around it. A few of the tables were occupied. One had a cookie-cutter family of blondes. Another had an elderly couple that were passing small condiment packets back and forth. Kevin, Mallory, and Ryan sat at a table in the very middle.

Ryan saw me first as I approached the table. A small smile spread across his face, which he seemed to try and hide immediately. Mallory and Kevin were deep in conversation about something. As I got closer, I realized it was about the show *Lost*.

"You can't spend six years setting up mysteries and then not answer 90% of them!" Mallory said, gesturing incredulously up in the air with her hands. "I mean, what is that?!"

Kevin leaned forward, tapping on the table with a finger to emphasize each word, "It was never about the science behind it, which you'd know if you paid attention to the central themes of the show."

"What 'central themes'?" Mallory replied, air quotes and all.

"Faith versus Science! John Locke versus Jack Shephard! It was always about that."

"So friggin' what?!"

"It ended being about the characters and their journey, not about the science behind how it all happened."

"But how does *that* make it about faith?" Mallory asked, leaning back in her chair and crossing her hands over her chest. "It was—hey, Peter." Kevin turned his head towards me as I reached the table. He was wearing a light blue button down that was hanging loose outside his jeans. There was a dark blue necktie tied loosely around his neck and his shirt sleeves were rolled up to the elbow.

"What's up, mister?" Mallory was dressed in a maroon shirt and jeans, her dark hair pulled back from her eyes. "How was church?"

"Pretty good," I replied, sitting down across from Ryan in his purple t-shirt and khaki pants. "The guy that sat behind me didn't have the best voice for the hymns."

Mallory laughed, "Oh gosh, there was a guy in front of me who fell asleep and every time we stood for a hymn I would sing really loudly above his ear. Somehow he didn't wake up till the end."

"I've seen him sleeping in the back before." Kevin added.

"So, what do you guys do here?" I asked.

"Well," Mallory said, "It sounds kind of stupid, but we've been meeting here and rating different food items from the various restaurants."

Kevin leaned in, "It started with fries. We wanted to do a side-by-side taste testing of them and see which one we thought was best."

"McDonald's." Ryan said, finally speaking up.

"That hasn't been settled on yet," Kevin replied. "After fries, we did chicken nuggets and then cheeseburgers."

"Wendy's was the obvious winner for nuggets." Mallory added, pointing at the sign behind her head. "Cheeseburgers was a tough mountain to climb."

Ryan patted his stomach.

"What's today?" I asked.

"Milkshakes!" Mallory replied, shaking her fingers in the air like she was doing magic.

"Awesome."

"We have to ask though," Kevin said, leaning close, "Do you think you're up for the challenge? This isn't an endeavor for the faint of heart. We're going to be consuming a lot of calories over the next hour. This isn't a time to be watching your girlish figure."

I laughed, "I'll do my best to not let you down."

With that, we got up and made our way to the left side of the semi-circle to start at the beginning of the line with McDonald's. We decided that we would use chocolate as our flavor choice for all of them so that our results would be more accurate. Moving through the line of restaurants (skipping the two Asian restaurants that didn't serve milkshakes), we procured our eight shakes. We alternated paying and I noticed that whenever Kevin's turn came around Mallory would watch him take out his cash with a look of concern on her face.

When we made it back to our table, we all began to trade the milkshakes back and forth. After taking a sip of one we would rate them on a scale of one to ten on four different categories: thickness, flavor, texture, and aftertaste. We had made small charts on our napkins, leaving space for additional comments at the bottom. No words were exchanged as we took long sips from the various colored straws.

As I sipped at a chocolate shake from Hardees, I glanced over at Ryan who was sitting across from me. He was filling in one of the categories on his napkin, his left hand holding the flimsy paper straight on the table. Looking up from the napkin, he reached to the middle of the table where the eight shakes were clustered and lifted the one from Potbelly's to his mouth. Taking a long sip, he placed the cup back down on the table and brought his hand to his jeans to wipe the sweat from the cup against his thigh.

Mallory, at my right, had finished first and was lifting a cheddar covered fry to her mouth, pulling the strings of cheese away as she bit into it.

To my left, at the end of the table, was Kevin, working thoroughly on his chart. As soon as he wrote a number down, he would erase it, putting another in its place. His fingertips rubbed at the tip of his chin as he worked.

When we were finished, Mallory took our charts and configured the results. The winner: Potbelly's.

"No contest," she said, picking up the Potbelly's cup and giving it a slurp.

"This was a lot easier than the cheeseburgers." Kevin replied.

"I didn't realize you could mess up a milkshake, but today I was proven wrong." I added, watching Mallory lean back in her chair and lift her hands to readjust her ponytail. "So how long have you guys known each other?"

Kevin furrowed his brow and twisted his mouth to the side as if he were thinking. "I met Mallory in . . . October of our sophomore year. We had a class together. Then we met Ryan a couple months later, I think. Mallory and her family started going to my church last year. It's been cheeseburgers and chicken nuggets ever since."

I looked from Kevin to Mallory, "Are your parents friends, too?"

Mallory pressed her lips together and looked across the table at Kevin. I turned to watch him glance down at his hands as they pressed into a napkin on the table. His lips parted and he took a breath.

"My parents aren't here anymore." He said, quickly looking up at me and giving me a brief smile before looking back down at his hands. "Two and a half years ago, my mom died of cancer. It started in her lungs and it just went everywhere. My dad had a really rough time after it happened and he, uh . . ." Kevin sighed heavily, lifting a hand and rubbing it over his jaw, "He took some stuff while I was at school." He was silent for a moment. "I live with my older brother now."

My stomach dropped. It was unimaginable. I had never known anyone who had lost their parents. Just the thought of it made my chest hurt and I couldn't even imagine how it would be from Kevin's perspective. There was a strained look on his face as he said it. His jaw was tight, and he kept swallowing, his throat clenching and unclenching. He looked like he was in pain.

"I'm so sorry," I said slowly. "I don't . . . I didn't mean . . ."

Kevin looked up and smiled, tight, but not sad. "It's okay. There's no way you could have known. Seriously, don't feel bad. Please."

It was silent for a few moments. I looked over at Ryan who was watching Kevin, staring at his face. He looked worried.

"Hey," Mallory said, breaking the silence. "Let's go walk around. That weird antique store is calling my name."

We walked along the upper level for a while. A lot of the stores and shops in the Haverty mall weren't big businesses. We had a Macy's and a Barnes & Noble and stores like that, but there were also some smaller, independent places. Like the place Mallory wanted to go to.

"I love this store. It's so random and kind of out of place." Mallory said as she led us into a small, dimly lit shop in the northwest corner of the mall. It was called *Corina's*. As soon as we walked through the glass doorway, the musky odor of old furniture hit my nose. Just inside the door was an area set up to look like someone's living room, a dusty couch and tall wingback chairs forming a semicircle around a marble coffee table. Behind this display was a variety of other furniture pieces, ranging from coatracks to headboards and nightstands. Most of the light in the shop came from lamps that were placed atop different pieces, shining just enough light to show off the woodwork without revealing any potential flaws.

"Isn't this stuff so pretty?" Mallory asked, as she led us through the maze of furniture.

"I'm pretty sure this is the same stuff that was here last time we came." Kevin said, scrunching up his face as we passed a particularly dusty end table.

"So?" Mallory responded.

"So, I don't think they ever actually sell anything."

"Of course they have. How would they stay in business if they didn't ever sell anything?"

Once we passed the maze of furniture, we reached a small checkout desk. There was a tall man standing behind it who looked to be in his early thirties. He had short blonde hair and a large, lean-muscled body. Mallory approached the desk.

"Hey, Mike, how's it going?" she said.

His mouth turned downwards in an overdramatic frown, "Oh, it's simply morbid, madam. I'm absolutely wasting away in this hole of mine. Corina has me working twenty-five hours a day, eight days a week. What's a man to do?"

"I'm sure some lovely boy will come and sweep you off your tired feet and take you away from all of this!" she replied, spreading her arm out to gesture at the store around them. "Got any new stuff in?"

Mike lost the drama and sat down on a stool behind the register, "Couple books, another Minolta. Most of the stuff we've been getting lately has been clothes." He picked up a tiny screwdriver that was sitting atop the register. "We got a watch in last week that I'm trying to get working again. I tried the battery, but it seems to be something in the mechanics."

"Well, I'll leave you to it. Don't work too hard. You're too pretty for that." Mallory replied, turning and walking away around a large wardrobe.

"That's what they all say. Then they leave." Mike called after us as we followed Mallory.

On the other side of the wardrobe was a clearing where large racks of clothes and bookshelves lined the walls. At the back wall of the shop was a doorway with a fitting room sign above it. There was a small skylight in the middle of the ceiling, sunlight shining through. Mallory paced around the area, glancing through the racks of clothing and books. Kevin sat down on a bench that was set up near the fitting rooms and pulled out his phone. I looked over the shelves of books, followed by Ryan. He reached up and pulled an old copy of *The Picture of Dorian Grey* off a shelf.

"Oh," I said, looking over his shoulder at the hardback book, "Have you read that one?"

"No," he replied, his voice small. "Have you?"

"Yeah, it's really good. It's one of my favorites actually."

Ryan opened the book and flipped through the pages slowly. Closing it, he held on to it as we continued to look. We stopped at a shelf that had several old pictures on it and a few old cameras. I reached up and pulled down a black Canon that was slightly dusty but looked like it was still in good condition.

"Oh my gosh, I love that one."

Mallory came up next to me, looking down at the camera. She took it from my hands and lifted it to her eye, pointing it over at Kevin who was obliviously staring at his phone. "This one's really good. I have one of this same model and it's not quite in as good a condition as this one. Mine has a small scratch on the viewfinder." She handed the camera back to me, "Do you like photography?"

I shrugged, "I've never really tried it out before except for quick pictures at family gatherings."

"You should get this." she said, lifting the tag to check the price. "It's only thirty dollars which is really good for this one. I could show you how to use it."

"Yeah, sure. That'd be really cool." I lifted the strap and placed it over my shoulder.

I walked back to the front where Mike was squinting at the back of a silver watch. He looked up when I placed the camera on the counter.

"This look fixed to you?" he held up the watch so I could see the face. The only movement was the second hand which was twitching slightly.

"Completely." I replied.

"Good. I knew I could do it." He tossed the watch to the side and picked up the camera. "Any chance you'd be interested in an oak nightstand? I could give you the pair for $100."

"I think I'm okay for now, but thanks."

"You sure? What about for $50? I won't go lower than $10."

I laughed as I pushed my debit card across the counter. Mike swiped it and handed it back.

"Want a bag with your coatrack?"

"Nah, I think I'll just carry it out. Thanks though."

Mike reached down below the counter and lifted his hand back up to show a roll of film. "This was in the box with the camera. Want me to load it up for you?"

"Sure, thanks."

He loaded up the camera and handed it back with a receipt.

As I walked away, I heard him say, "Tell all your friends about our fine headboard selection!"

When I got to the back again, Kevin and Ryan were sitting on the bench. Kevin was leaned forward with his elbows on his knees, black curls falling over his forehead as he typed out a text. Ryan sat next to him; knees pulled up to his chest with *Dorian Grey* open across them. I watched as his eyes moved slowly across the pages.

"Where's Mallory?" I asked, looking around the space.

"She's trying on a dress." Kevin replied, looking up from his phone.

At that moment, Mallory stepped out of the doorway of the fitting rooms. She had on a bright yellow sun dress that went down to her knees. Her dark brown hair was swept over one shoulder as she stepped in front of a small mirror that was standing in the corner of the room.

"How does it look?" she asked, turning so she could see the back.

"You look perfect." Kevin replied.

I watched as he stood up, watching her look at herself in the mirror. His eyes seemed fixed on Mallory, his lips slightly parted as his chest rose and fell with every breath. She turned and looked at him, fidgeting with the hem at her right knee.

Ryan leaned forward, placing his feet on the floor again, "I like it."

Mallory glanced at Kevin once more before turning back to look in the mirror. "It's only twelve dollars. I think I'm going to get it."

She stepped away from the mirror and walked past Kevin toward the fitting rooms. Kevin's head turned as she passed him before he sat back down.

There was something odd about the way they had looked at each other. They were obviously into each other and knew it. But there was something about how they'd responded, seemingly upfront about their attraction, but sad at the same time. Mallory had almost frowned when she'd looked back at herself in the mirror, Kevin looking down at his shoes after sitting down again.

"Wait," I said, before Mallory could pass through the doorway. She turned back to me, the light from the window in the ceiling shining over her left side.

I lifted my camera to my eye, turning the lens until it was focused on her. She gave me a half-smile, her hands smoothing across her stomach and around her sides.

Click.

7

"Well, what do you want me to do, Melanie? Huh? Do you want me to give you an itinerary for my day? Plan out every fucking move I'm going to make so you know ahead of time? Is that what you want?"

"No, Saul, I don't need you to make an itinerary for me and please don't swear at me."

They had been going at it for twenty minutes. Although, several of the minutes were spent with my mom trying to get my father to respond to her.

It had started like it normally did, with my father coming in late when he had said he would be home for dinner. My mom called him on it, saying that if he was going to be late, all she needed him to do was text her, just a simple heads-up. She said it in a nice tone, not scolding or nagging, but my father had immediately taken offense. This had begun the evenings fight.

I went up into my room like usual to hide out and do homework, but they had brought the battle upstairs this time, into their bedroom. Even with my door shut and my record player on, I could still hear every word from my spot in the closet.

"It sounds like that's what I'm going to have to do if I want some peace when I walk in the door. Otherwise, I'm going to have you down my throat the second I get home." My father's deep voice came through the wall, thick and accusing.

My mom responded, her calmer, more defensive voice slipping under my door, "I'm sorry, Saul. Okay? I'm sorry. I should never have said anything. Next time, I'll just leave your plate in the microwave. I just won't say anything. You can just come home whenever you want."

"No, I can't. You can't help yourself. You won't be able to leave me alone. If you can't say something you won't know what to do with yourself. It'll drive you crazy. You have to be nagging me about something, otherwise you won't have a purpose."

"Why are you being like this, Saul?"

"Like what?" I could almost hear the spit in his voice.

"Like this. So mean. You're just being mean now, Saul."

"Shut up, Melanie. I'm not being mean. Don't try and turn this around on me."

"Why not? That's what you've been doing. You walk in the door late, without giving me any kind of notice, and I say one thing to you and you make me out to be some bitch of a wife."

"Well, that's what you're being!"

I pulled the door of my closet closed a little more, not caring about hearing my music playing. I just wanted to get away from their voices. Just the sound of them created a tightness in my chest. My stomach twisted into a knot that wouldn't release until they had stopped.

Still, their voices made it through.

"How am I being like that? How am I being a bitch? Is it such a bad thing for me to want to know whether or not my husband is going to be home for dinner? Why is that so wrong?"

"Because I can't fucking tell you all the time when I'm going to be home!" He was starting to yell now. My stomach twisted tighter. My fingers gripping the edge of my notebook.

"I asked you not to swear at me like that, Saul. Please at least give me that." I could feel her sigh through the door. "Do you think I like this? Do you think I like fighting with you? I don't. I hate it. I hate getting yelled at by the man who is supposed to be my husband."

There were a few moments of silence. I sat still, waiting nervously to see if they would just let it be done then. Silence rang in my ears, my head hurting.

My mother's voice drifted softly through the wall, "Saul, why can't you ju- "

"I should just leave."

My breath caught in my throat.

"Saul."

"I should just leave. You're obviously not happy with anything I do." His voice was calmer now, tired.

"Don't say that, Saul. That's not true. You're not going to leave." I could hear the uncertainty in her voice. Would he leave? Was that an option?

"What if I did? You'd be happier that way."

"No, I wouldn't, Saul! I would not be happier. Why do you think it would make me happy to have my husband leave me?" There were tears in her voice now. I could imagine her face getting red as the tears slid down her cheeks. She would pick up a tissue and hold it to her eyes for several seconds. I had seen her cry so many times that I could visualize it instantly.

"You would be happier without me, and you know it." For once, he didn't sound mean or spiteful. His words were slow, careful, like he wasn't just firing off insults or jabs.

"Saul. You are my husband. I love you. I don't want you to leave. I just want us to be happy together."

"I don't know if that's possible anymore."

Her words were muffled slightly through her tears, "It is possible. Just please don't say you're going to leave. Please don't ever say that again."

It was silent again for several minutes. I wondered what was happening, what they were doing. Were they hugging? Did they even hug anymore? I couldn't remember the last time I had seen them hug. Maybe when I was little, but not in a long time.

Did my father really want to leave? It seemed like something that he was considering. The way his voice became calmer, his words sounding more deliberate. It wasn't just something he picked up and threw at her like all his other comments. He had thought about this one.

"I'm going to bed now." His voice was so quiet, I almost couldn't make it out.

"I love you, Saul. I really do. Please know that." My mother didn't sound like she was crying anymore. Her voice came through weighed down with exhaustion.

"I know, Melanie."

There was a soft click as a door shut and I heard the water begin moving through the pipes in the walls. My father was taking a shower.

I turned to look at the wall of my closet. One of Brooke's writings stood out at me.

I'm so tired

I crept out of my closet and stepped over to the door of my room. Opening it just a couple inches, I peeked across the hall through their open doorway. I could see my mother sitting on the edge of her bed. Her hands were at her sides, resting on the rumpled sheets. She was looking at the floor, but her focus seemed to be lost somewhere. I could see the red of her cheeks, her mascara smeared in streaks beneath her eyes.

She looked broken, more broken than she usually was after one of their fights. I knew it was because of what he'd said, because she could hear the same thing I could. The seriousness in his voice. I wondered what she was thinking at that moment. Was she scared? Worried? Did she think he was actually considering it?

I shut the door and turned my back to it, slumping down on the floor. Yes, there had been something different about the way he said it, but did I think he would do it? The more I sat there and thought about it, the more I realized something. It was something that I thought about before, but now somehow knew it to be true.

I truly wanted him to do it.

8

A couple weeks after the mall, Mallory and I met up in Manchester Park so she could show me how to use the camera I bought. Ryan was at home and Kevin was working at his job at Foot Locker.

It was a sunny Saturday afternoon and kids were running around everywhere. A couple was sitting on a red and blue blanket under a tree while their kids played fetch with a white Labrador. There was a nice breeze as we strolled through the park, Mallory pointing out different tools on the camera.

"This one adjusts your ISO." she said, placing her finger on a large silver knob next to the viewfinder. "The darker your lighting situation, the higher your ISO has to be. Unless you have a flash. Given the sunlight and all the trees creating shadows, you can leave it at 400 for now." She lifted the camera, focused on a squirrel that was sitting on a branch nearby and clicked the shutter. "Yeah, 400 will work. The thing to remember about working with film as opposed to digital is that you only have a certain number of shots per roll. Since you can't see it until it's printed and film is rather expensive, you'll want to use your shots wisely. You don't want to spend an entire roll taking photos of a flower unless you feel confident about the images you're getting."

She handed me the camera and I looked around for something interesting to capture.

"You really know your stuff. How long have you been into photography?" I asked, lifting the camera to my eye, and focusing in on a golden retriever that was sitting beneath a tree next to a middle-aged man who was reading a newspaper. The dog was watching the Labrador intently as it ran back and forth a few yards away.

Click.

"I kinda got into it in middle school. I got a camera like yours at a yard sale and fell in love. There are albums full of photos in my room that have all kinds of different themes. There's family photos and nature photos and still life photos. It takes up two whole shelves."

"Are you going to try to do it professionally? Like go to school for it and stuff?"

"No, I need to be smart. Getting a job in the arts is so hard and being successful in the arts is even harder. I need to do something that I'll actually be able to get a job in and make some decent money."

I looked at her, the sunlight hitting her face and making her squint. "I mean, if you go to the right school, you'll have people that'll help you make your way in the field. They have good resources for that kind of thing."

"Yeah, but I want to be really successful. My mom always told me that by the time I get married, I should already be self-sufficient, that I should be able to bring just as much to the table as my husband can. I just don't see that happening with photography." She ran a hand through her hair, the long strands sliding across the collar of her white t-shirt.

Part of me admired her for making the smart choice, to choose financial stability over creative passion, but there was something sad about it, about having to give up that passion for stability.

Mallory's phone rang, pulling me from my thoughts. She pulled it out of her pocket and looked at the screen before answering.

"Hello?" she said. "What? . . . He did it again? Ok, we're on our way."

She put the phone back in her pocket and looked at me, her face suddenly pale. "We have to go."

I followed her as she began walking back to her car. "What's going on? Who was that?"

She stopped at her car door, opening it as she spoke. "It was Ryan's Mom. He tried to kill himself again."

My heart thumped in my chest. "Did you say 'again'?"

It smelled like antiseptic as Mallory and I ran down the florescent hallway to Ryan's room. It had been pills. His mother hadn't said what kind, just that it was a handful. On the car ride over, Mallory had told me about the last time he'd done this. It had been pills then, too.

When we reached his room, the door was ajar. The lights were off as we entered. Dim bars of sun light shone through the lowered blinds, breaking up the darkness. There wasn't much furniture in the room besides the bed, side table, and a cheap recliner. A small TV hung from a spot high on the wall. Ryan was laying on his side on the bed, facing us. As my eyes adjusted to the darkness, I could see him looking at us. He looked away when our eyes met.

"Hey, buddy" Mallory greeted him softly. Her voice attempted casualty but failed to cover her sympathy. She stood by the bed and took his hand, rubbing slow circles over the top. His eyes moved from their joined hands to her face.

"I know, it's okay. Where are your parents?"

His lips parted just enough for words to escape, "Home. Picking up stuff. My dad's on a flight back from his conference." He looked back down at their hands and followed the motion of her thumb.

I could see Mallory's back straighten, going into Mom mode.

"Okay, well, do you want something to eat? We could go grab you something from the cafeteria. Or we could go pick you up a burger somewhere. The hospital food doesn't sound very appetizing. Or maybe you just— "

She stopped as a pair of sneakers could be heard running down the hall. A second later, Kevin's silhouette shadowed the doorway. He took two broad steps in, looked over at the bed and launched. Lifting one foot up, he pushed himself atop the bed. One knee fell on either side of Ryan, both hands coming up and turning him onto his back. His heavy breathing filled the room. Even in the darkness, I could see his body vibrating with rage. Ryan immediately started crying.

"You promised me!" Kevin spat through gritted teeth, "You PROMISED ME you wouldn't do this again!" He pressed his hands into the mattress on either side of Ryan's head. Mallory backed away slowly to stand by me. "Why did you do it? WHY?"

I hadn't seen Kevin angry before. He didn't seem like the kind of person who could *get* this angry. This wasn't the kind of situation that would call for that kind of fury. Ryan didn't need that right now. I took a step forward, but Mallory grabbed my wrist. When I looked back, she just shook her head. I stepped back.

Kevin still hovered over Ryan as he sobbed, "Answer me! Why did you do it?"

Through tears, "I don't know."

"Yes, you do. You didn't just do it. People don't try to end their life for no reason.

"Because it doesn't matter."

Kevin slammed his fist down on the bed to the right of Ryan's head. He cried harder. "How dare you say that? It doesn't matter? What doesn't matter? *You*?" I could almost see Kevin's nostrils flaring in the dim light. "I can't believe you did this again. You told me you were feeling better. You said the depression wasn't as bad now. I thought the medicine was helping." Kevin's words were starting to sound muffled. He was crying too. "Why didn't you tell me about this? You promised me you would let me know if you were feeling this way again."

Kevin sat back up on his heels, breathing deeply. Mallory stood at my side, unmoving. Her mouth was a firm line across her face. I watched them all and felt like there were things not being said. There was so much that I didn't know about them, about what they'd been through together.

Kevin leaned back down again, "This won't happen again. I can't take this again. Do you realize what this does to me? Do you know what it's like to get a call like that again? I couldn't breathe. I felt empty.

The second your mom said those words it was like someone had cut out my insides. It was like agony, but I couldn't feel anything because there was nothing. There's nothing without you. You've become a part of me now. You've become a part of all of us. Look at them." His hand came up to Ryan's jaw, turning his head towards us. Ryan's eyes locked with Mallory's, then mine. "You're a part of them now. They need you. You matter to them. Why would you leave that?"

Ryan's face scrunched as more tears slid down his cheek. The light from the doorway shone in his eyes.

Kevin turned Ryan back to him. He slowed his movements, gently brushing the tears away from Ryan's cheeks with the top of his fingers. "You're not going to do this again. I don't even want your promise this time. You'll take your medicine. You'll go to therapy. It won't happen again. Okay?" Ryan nodded slowly.

Moving back down the bed, Kevin stepped off and stood up. He walked over to us and pulled out his wallet. "Here," he handed us a $20 bill, "Go get us all some hamburgers and milkshakes. He'll want chocolate."

He walked back over by the bed where Ryan was starting to sit up. Grabbing the pillow from the chair behind him, he propped it up so Ryan could lean against it. He then sat down in the recliner by the bed and picked up the TV remote.

As Mallory and I turned to go, I looked back at them watching the TV. Blue light illuminated their tired faces. They both stared at the screen, neither really seeing what was on it. Ryan sat against his pillow, eyes hooded. Kevin's hand came up and wrapped around Ryan's forearm. It stayed there, a friend in the dark, as we left the room.

We were on the way back to the hospital when she told me. She'd been quiet while we picked up the food, driving with her elbow against the window ledge and biting her thumb.

"You need to know what happened to Ryan," she said as we drove back, fast food bags in my lap. "I wasn't going to say anything because it's not my story to tell, but you should know if this is happening again."

"Okay." I wasn't sure if I wanted her to tell me. This seemed like Ryan's business, like something only he should tell me. It felt like a betrayal of his trust for Mallory to share this with me, but she was so shaken by what had happened at the hospital. And, admittedly, I did want to know.

She sighed and pressed her lips together before speaking. "Ryan got bullied pretty hard at his old high school in Indiana. His mom said he was the kind of kid that made an easy target because he was so small and quiet. It wasn't too bad at first, just some name-calling and taunting, but apparently it escalated quickly."

She was quiet for a moment, her hands gripping the steering wheel. I watched her eyes as she looked out at the road in front of us, the passing cars. Her silence made me nervous.

When she finally spoke again, her words sounded slow and careful. "His parents don't know if the kids who were messing with him actually knew he was gay or not. Maybe they didn't care. Either way . . . one night, after a football game, a couple guys threw a bag over his head and tossed him in the back seat of their car. They drove him out to a field somewhere and poured ice water over his head and beat the shit out of him. Before they were done, they put a gun to his head, or what he believes to be a gun, it could have been anything, and threatened to shoot him if he didn't say he was a faggot."

I felt sick. I knew things like that happened, that there were people like that in the world, but for people like that to happen to Ryan? That kind of cruelty? Ryan was kind and sweet and good. It broke my heart to think about someone trying to silence that.

We had reached the hospital and Mallory pulled into a parking space. Pulling the key out of the ignition, she turned in her seat to look at me.

"Peter, you need to know about this because Ryan needs people around him who are going to help. He needs real friends right now." She looked me in the eyes as she spoke. "We really like you, Peter, but Ryan has to come first right now. If you're not up for something like this, it's okay. We won't think less of you."

"No," I replied, my eyes locking on hers, so she knew I was serious. "I'm all in. I want to help him."

"Are you sure?"

"Yes. I want Ryan to be happy. He deserves to be happy."

Mallory watched me for just a moment longer before reaching over and taking the fast-food bags from my lap. "You get the shakes."

I got out of the car and followed her inside to find our friends.

9

I didn't see Ryan for the next week. Mallory and Kevin said he was spending a lot of time at home and that he had started going to therapy again. I really wanted Ryan to be okay. Every time I thought about him, my mind kept going back to what Mallory had told me. No one deserved that kind of pain and cruelty. Especially someone like Ryan.

That Thursday, my mom and I went to the grocery store after school. She wanted to get some things to cook dinner that night and I just wanted to avoid working on my story. I was almost done with all the other edits Mrs. Stroud had given me and was finally going to have to focus on the ending. I'd been thinking about it all week but was still struggling with it.

"We should have burgers tonight. How does that sound?" she asked as we walked down the bread aisle. The wheels of the cart squeaked as they rolled along the scuffed-up floor.

"Sure, that sounds fine." I replied, grabbing a pack of burger buns off the top shelf.

"Your dad could put them on the grill, or I can if he's not home in time."

"He probably won't be." I said.

She sighed, "You never know."

Sometimes, when she said things like this, I wondered where she was getting her hope from. Yes, things had been okay for a couple weeks, but that didn't mean they couldn't change at the drop of a hat. Part of me didn't want to see her getting her hopes up because it would just make her hurt more when she was let down.

"We should go see a movie this weekend. I think there's a new Tina Fey one out." She said, as we turned down another aisle to find the burgers. Her red hair was pulled back in a ponytail and she reached up to adjust it with one hand as we walked.

"Yeah, that could be fun."

"I think your father has to work most of the weekend, so it'll probably be just us." Stopping in front of the raw meats, she picked up a package with two burgers and put it into our cart.

"Why are you only getting two?" I asked.

"It was Ronnie's birthday today, so we had a cake for him at work. I'm just going to eat veggies tonight." She sounded perfectly fine with this decision, but it still made me sad for her. This was another one of her favorite meals that she was planning to cook and not eat. I wanted to tell her that it was okay to splurge a little, especially since we hadn't had burgers in a while, but I knew that she would say she'd already splurged with the cake and needed to cut back.

She turned the cart down another aisle, and we headed to the front to check out.

That Saturday, we all went over to Kevin's house. He lived in a small apartment complex about a mile from my house. There were three buildings with four apartments in each. Kevin lived in apartment 2A with his older brother, Jeremy.

Mallory's car was already there when I pulled up. I got out and headed up the steps to Kevin's place. There was a small potted flower sitting next to the black door when I got to the top floor. A rusted metal doorknocker hung from hooks just beneath the peephole. I knocked twice and waited till Kevin came to the door.

"Hey!" he said, stepping aside so I could enter. The door opened into a small living room. There was a faded blue couch that looked like it had a few holes in the fabric. In front of the couch was a round coffee table that had a couple coasters on it and nothing else. On the other side of the table were two wooden chairs and a small television sitting on a black ottoman. There was a doorway across from the front door that led to a small kitchen with white cabinets and black countertops. To the left of the door was a short hallway with three doors leading off from it.

"Welcome," Kevin said as he shut the door behind me.

"I like your apartment," I said as he led me into the kitchen. It was very small, cabinets and countertops along two walls. The wall to the right had a washer and dryer hooked up with a shelf holding detergent and various storage containers up above. A small rectangular table that sat four people with limited leg room took up half the floor space.

Mallory and Ryan were sitting at the table, a bag of chips between them. Mallory's hair was pulled back in a loose bun, strands of hair hanging down around her face. Ryan was wrapped in a cardigan as he lifted a chip and tossed it into his mouth. I hadn't seen him since that day at the hospital. He surprisingly looked okay, almost like he did before it happened. The only difference was that he looked more tired. Mallory told me he had been sleeping a lot. His eyes were a little dark as he looked up at me. He didn't smile, but there was a light in his eyes that made me feel like he was glad to see me. I wanted to ask how he was feeling and if he was having an urge to repeat what he did.

"Peter, where have you been?" Mallory asked as I sat down at the table. "Ryan and I have almost eaten this whole bag. Do you realize how much candy I'm gonna have to eat to even out my salty to sweet ratio?"

I laughed, "I'm sure you'll manage somehow."

"Oh, I'll manage. I just want you to be aware of the amount of food I'm going to consume this afternoon so that you don't get too shocked."

"So, what are we gonna do today?" Kevin asked, sitting down in the empty chair at the table.

"You mean besides eat?" Mallory responded.

Kevin laughed, "*Yes*, besides eat."

"I don't really care what we do," Mallory said as she leaned back in her chair. "Anything to get my mind off of next year."

"Been working on your applications?" I asked.

"All. Freakin'. Morning." she replied, rolling her eyes.

"What'd you put as your major?"

"Physical Therapy." Mallory leaned her elbows on the table and put her face in her hands.

"Why Physical Therapy?"

"My Uncle works for a PT clinic and said that he could probably help me find a job when I graduate."

"Ryan." Mallory and I turned to look at Kevin who was staring across the table at Ryan. Ryan was sitting with his arms around him. There was a frown on his face as he stared down at the table, his eyes looking dazed as he raised his head to look back at Kevin.

"You okay, buddy?" Kevin asked.

Ryan nodded quickly. "Yeah, I'm fine." He sat up a little straighter in his chair and pulled his sweater tighter around his abdomen.

"You sure? Do you want us to take you home or go out somewhere?" Kevin's tone sounded concerned, but much calmer than he'd been at the hospital.

"No, I wanna stay here. I'm okay. I promise." He looked from Kevin to Mallory, worry in his eyes.

Kevin watched him a moment before responding, "Okay. So let's find something to do today."

Ryan looked over at me, lifting a hand to rub at the side of his face. I smiled at him, hoping he would feel more comfortable.

There was a sound of footsteps behind us and I turned to see a man walk into the room. This was clearly Jeremy. He looked just like Kevin, only older. He was around Kevin's height and his black hair was straight instead of curly and had little flickers of grey throughout. He was wearing a plaid button down and jeans and had a messenger bag hanging from his shoulder.

"Hey, Jer, this is Peter. I told you about him, right?" Kevin said, turning in his chair to look back at him.

Jeremy placed a coffee mug in the sink and turned to us, seeing me and nodding. "Hey, it's nice to meet you. I'm Jeremy." His voice was deep and a little scratchy. He extended his hand to me and I shook it, his grip firm without crushing me.

"Nice to meet you, too." I said as he turned back around and pulled an aluminum water bottle out of the cabinet and began filling it at the sink.

"Where ya headed?" Kevin asked him.

"I gotta go into my office. I left some papers there that I need to grade, and I might just grade them while I'm there so I don't have to bring them back home with me."

"Jeremy teaches at the community college." Kevin said to me.

"What do you teach?" I asked.

He turned off the faucet and screwed the lid back on the bottle. "19th Century Literature."

"That sounds interesting."

He chuckled, "Well, you should tell that to my students. So, what are you guys doing today?"

"Some witchcraft, animal sacrifice, maybe defiling your brother later." Mallory responded casually.

"Just make sure he's healthy enough to go to work tomorrow. I'll see you guys later."

"Bye, Jer." Kevin called as Jeremy walked out of the room followed by the sound of the front door opening and closing.

I turned to Kevin, "He seems cool."

"Yeah, he's great. He teaches class three times a week in addition to stocking groceries at Jewel and writing for the newspaper. I don't know how he does it all without going crazy. I'm only working *one* job and going to school, and *I* feel stressed all the time."

"Why does he have to work so many jobs?" I asked.

"Because we just don't have enough money to get by. When my parents died, they had a lot of credit card debt, so the majority of my mom's life insurance went to pay that off and then for the funeral.

Jeremy moved into the house, but we could only stay there a few more months because the mortgage was too expensive, and we couldn't pay it. The bank ended up foreclosing. That's when we moved here. He was already teaching at the college, but he took on the other two jobs because it still wasn't enough. I've been using most of my paycheck from the shoe store to help out, too."

It was such a difficult situation for them to be in, having to work constantly just to survive. It sounded like Kevin and Jeremy never had a moment to really breathe, to feel secure. I thought about the fact that both of my parents were not only still alive, but both had good jobs that allowed us to live comfortably in our house. I wondered what my life would be like if I was in Kevin's position, how I would feel having to always worry about making enough money to pay the bills. It seemed like a rough way to live, and I hated that Kevin was having to go through that all the time.

"Anyway," Kevin said, glancing at Ryan again as he leaned forward on the table. "For the last time, what are we gonna do?"

We ended up watching a movie on Kevin's couch, Mallory hugging a bag of gummy worms she had brought with her. The movie was a lame Hollywood action movie that we made fun of the whole time. Ryan sat at the end of the couch, leaning his head on the arm. Like Kevin and Mallory, I kept looking over at him throughout the movie, checking on him to see if he was okay. Every now and then I would see him smile or laugh at one of our jokes. Other times, he was just intently watching the movie.

Around 5 o'clock, Mallory got a text from her parents asking her to go by the grocery store to pick some stuff up for dinner. Ryan was supposed to be home by six because his mom and dad were cooking a big dinner and his aunt was coming over. Mallory wasn't going to have time to get him home and get to the store before her mom needed her back, so I offered to give him a ride.

He was quiet as we got in my car and pulled out of the parking lot. His hands stayed in his lap, his body not taking up any more space than necessary. He looked very reserved as he sat there, back straight, not making a sound.

I turned to look at him when we got to a stoplight, "Do you mind if I ask if you're okay?"

"Yeah," he replied, his soft voice filling the silence of the car. "I'm fine."

I wasn't sure if there was a right way to ask what I wanted to ask him. "I mean, are you okay after, you know, everything?"

He was silent again for a second. "I'm okay. I'm better now. I shouldn't have done what I did. It was . . . it wasn't the right choice."

His voice was calm and clear as he spoke, and I wondered if he actually believed what he said or if he was just repeating what everyone had been telling him.

As I pulled away from the stoplight I said, "I want you to know that even though we haven't known each other very long, you can talk to me if you need to. I know I'm not Kevin or Mallory, but I'm here if you need me because I don't want you to get to a point where you feel like you have to do that again. You're really cool and I just . . . I'm just really glad it didn't work. I'm glad you're still here."

"You can go right here," he said, pointing at the next turn.

He was silent as we drove the rest of the way to his house, except for the directions he gave me. I worried that I had overstepped some kind of boundary or crossed a line. I hoped I hadn't made him uncomfortable.

We finally pulled up outside his home, a nice brick two-story house with a big wooden door. There was a small sign in the front yard promoting some political candidate who I'd never heard of. There was a light on in one of the first-floor windows and the drapes were pulled back. I could see a tall man moving around a large table in a room with red walls.

"That's my dad." Ryan said, looking at the window. He opened the car door but stopped before getting out. Half-turning back without looking at me he said, "Thank you for what you said."

I felt a small amount of relief, "Yeah, of course. I just don't want you to feel sad or upset. I want you to feel okay with me."

His eyes were on the floor mat at his feet, "I know I don't talk a lot. I think you're cool too, though, and I, uh, I really like hanging out with you."

I could see him glance at me quickly out of the corner of his eyes. This was the most he'd said to me at one time since we'd met, and I couldn't help feeling like it was a small victory.

"I like hanging out with you too."

He looked up at his house, "Thank you for the ride home."

"You're welcome. Anytime." I watched as he got out of the car and shut the door gently behind him. He walked across his front yard to the door, unlocking it and turning to give me a little wave before stepping inside.

I pulled away from the curb and drove off down the street. He was speaking to me more. That was something. Maybe he was finally starting to look at me as a friend, like Kevin and Mallory. I wanted that. I wanted him to trust me and to feel safe with me. He was so sad all the time, so weighed down in his mind, and I wanted to be someone who could relieve some of that weight for him. I thought about that little smile and how beautiful it had looked on his face. There was something so wonderful about seeing him like that. I was going to make him smile again, as often as I possibly could. I was determined.

10

I opened the glass-paned door of the Empty Cup and stepped inside, the cold November air whooshing behind me as the door closed with a gentle click.

Scanning the room, I found Kevin and Ryan sitting at a table to my left, right next to one of the front windows. I could see that they were already deep into a game of chess, pawns and rooks scattered across the board. Kevin was rubbing his chin, his free hand in a tight, concentrated fist against his denim-clad thigh. His navy-blue sweatshirt was zipped halfway, exposing his black *West Haverty High School* t-shirt. Ryan sat across from him, hands together in his khaki covered lap, shoulders slouched comfortably. He was wrapped in a burgundy sweater that looked half a size too big on him. His knees bounced gently beneath the table, a nervous tick I had noticed was a signature of his.

I ordered myself a hot chocolate and walked over to where they were sitting. Like many of the others, our table was small. I liked that. I liked the closeness. I had never had friends to be close to before.

As I approached, I watched Kevin reach up and close his fingers over the top of one of his rooks, moving it forward three spaces, taking one of Ryan's pawns in the process. Without thinking, Ryan picked up one of his bishops (both still in play) and moved it diagonally across the board, directly to where Kevin's rook now sat. He put the bishop in its place and dropped the captured rook next to his brown paper coffee cup beside the board. His hands fell back to his knees.

"How did you do that?" Kevin asked, one hand hovering mid-air.

I could see Ryan's chest filling with breath, like he was about to go into a long explanation of how he made the move and what mistakes Kevin made that allowed him to make it. He wasn't going to explain, he wasn't going to say anything at all. Ryan lifted his hands from his still bouncing knees and brought the bishop back to its original position and took it through the move again, letting Kevin watch and see where his choice had brought him. There was a small glimmer of pride in his eyes, the corners of his mouth twitching up just the slightest bit. He seemed okay, like today was one of the good days. He'd been going to therapy twice a week since the incident. Judging from his improved appearance over the past few weeks, it seemed to be helping. Kevin said we still needed to watch him though. Therapy wasn't a quick fix, especially for someone like Ryan.

Kevin gave a deep chuckle, "Damn, how did I not see that?" His hand came back up to rub against the thin layer of stubble that covered his chin. He squinted at the board for a moment before making a countermove.

"Hey, guys."

"Hey!" Kevin and Ryan looked up at me as I approached the table and sat down in one of the two empty chairs, mine facing the window. I saw Ryan glance at me quickly before focusing back on the board, a smile playing on his lips.

I took a warm sip of my drink, "Where's Mallory?"

"Uh, I don't know." Kevin replied as he watched Ryan move his rook and take one of Kevin's pawns. "Damn it! —She texted me when I was picking up Ryan that she would be a little late."

We sat there for a while, Kevin and Ryan hunched over the chess board. Every few seconds, Kevin would release an exasperated sigh, Ryan glancing up at him with that smile. I watched them with a mix of amused fascination and the deepest sense of comfort. I had never had friends like these, the kind with whom words were unnecessary. We sat there in the small, warm coffee shop, the soft whir of espresso machines in our ears, and just existed together. We didn't need to fill the silence with deep conversations and witty jabs. It was fine to just be.

I like this, I want this to stay, I thought, watching Kevin pull up the sleeves of his sweatshirt and place his hands on his thighs in a failing attempt to gain some perspective on what was happening on the board, a perspective that Ryan seemed to naturally hold.

When Mallory finally arrived, she came rushing through the door, several patrons looking up at the cause of the sudden intrusion of cool air. Mallory turned her head frantically from the right side of the room to the left, her hair sweeping from one shoulder to the other, searching us out. When she spotted us, she quickly ran over to our table and sat down in the only remaining chair across from me. Her eyes were big orbs of brown as she looked from the chess board to each of our faces.

"So, I have news!" She flung her hand in the air between Kevin and Ryan's faces, snapping her fingers several times to gather their attention. She was ecstatic, her entire body was almost humming with an uncontrollable excitement that was more nervous than anything as she shifted around in her seat, unable to stay still, needing to tell her news and to tell it as soon as possible.

"All right, what?" Kevin didn't look happy about breaking his concentration, a sigh falling from his lips as he leaned back in his chair and turned to Mallory.

"Well," she paused, wide eyes moving across each of our faces for a moment, lingering a second longer on Kevin's. "I've met someone!" Her entire upper body shook as she said this, an anxious grin spreading across her face.

I turned to Kevin as I saw his shoulders slouch, his expression shifting from one of curiosity to one of concern.

"Wait, wait, wait, back up. Who did you meet?" Kevin's brow furrowed as he waited for a response.

"His name is Theo. He's been working as an office aid at my dad's firm. I had to stop by there this afternoon to give him his house keys—he'd left them at home—and as I was leaving, I ran into Theo in the elevator. We started talking and he said he'd seen me around the office a couple times before and by the time I realized what was going on we were already outside at my car." Her fingertips were curled around the edge of the tabletop as she told her story, each one jittering and clenching with every passing word. "He asked me if I was doing anything tonight and I told him I was meeting you guys, so he asked if I wanted to go to the diner and get a milkshake before I left to come here. We ended up going and I just completely lost track of time while we were talking and I'm so sorry I'm late, I swear I wasn't ditching you guys. Please don't be mad, I- "

"So you went out to dinner with some guy you've never met before?" Kevin's voice was heavy with concern. I didn't understand this attitude, but Mallory seemed to.

"It wasn't dinner, Kevin. It was just a milkshake. Besides, he works for my dad, it's not like he was a bum off the street."

"That doesn't mean *anything*."

"It's not like I went to his house. We went to the diner, a public place. There were people around, if he had done something to me than someone would have seen it. I'm not a child. He's a very nice guy, Kevin. I really liked him. He's polite and smart and he's enlisted in the Marines, so he'll be leaving in April fo- "

"Wait, you're interested in a guy who's leaving in six months? You might be starting a relationship with a guy and he's not even going to be here a year from now?"

Kevin's hands moved with every word, jumping into the air or spreading wide to emphasize his point. The dimples in his cheeks made shallow valleys in his face as his mouth hung open in question. I watched the muscles in his jaw flex, moving the skin of his cheek in taut ripples across his face. He didn't seem angry, but strangely defensive.

Mallory was beginning to get frustrated now. I could see her breathing increase, her chest rising a little faster as she looked up into Kevin's eyes, meeting him on his level. I turned to Ryan who wasn't looking at either of them. His eyes were on the board, moving back and forth between the king and queen. Worry covered his face. I wanted to reach out and put a hand on his arm, some small gesture that would help him feel more comfortable and at ease, but I wasn't sure if we were at a point in our friendship where that would be okay.

I turned back to Kevin and Mallory. They hadn't argued like this in front me before. I didn't know if they'd *ever* argued like this before. There had been little disagreements, little squabbles, but they had all been silly and playful. The way they were arguing now, though, made me think it wasn't the first time it had gotten this heated. They seemed to know their roles, when to cut in on the other, when to let the other rant. It all played out like a scripted argument in a television show.

"I never said anything about a relationship. I just said that we'd talked and I liked him. That doesn't mean he's my boyfriend. What does it matter anyway? I'm eighteen years old, I can date whoever the hell I want." Mallory's eyes were focused and harsh on Kevin's. "Is there a reason why I shouldn't date him?"

Kevin ignored her question, "Who is this guy? For all you know, this guy could just be using you before he leaves town. I'm afraid you're not thinking clearly."

Mallory's mouth fell open at this last remark. She almost laughed as she spoke again. "Thinking clearly? *Thinking clearly?* When have I ever been the kind of person who doesn't think clearly? I over-think every-thing! I plan things and second guess myself and constantly, *constantly,* make sure I'm making the right choice. I *always* think clearly. Just because I met the guy today doesn't mean that's changed."

Their voices were starting to rise now. I could see a couple people sitting at a nearby table glance over at us.

"Hey, uh, guys?" Mallory and Kevin looked over at me, the heat of the argument coloring their faces, and I nodded towards the other table. "You might wanna keep it down." I darted my eyes over towards Ryan and they both turned to look at him. His face was turned down towards his lap, a frown on his lips.

Mallory took a deep breath and got up from the table, "We'll be right back." She headed for the door. Shoving it open, she stepped out into the parking lot.

Kevin looked at Ryan for a moment. "We're okay, man. Don't worry." he said, before getting up and following her out.

The reflection of the light from the café in the glass obstructed my view slightly, but I could still see their hands and faces moving, silhouettes illuminated by a streetlamp several yards behind them. I couldn't hear what they were saying, but it was clearly still pretty heated. Kevin was saying something, his arms spread out at his sides as if he were waiting for her to come at him with her fists held high. Mallory had her finger back in his face as she spat words at him. She looked up at him, his extra two inches giving a surprisingly noticeable height difference. I looked over at Ryan, his eyes on the chess board, hands in his lap as one thumb ran over the nail of the other. He looked sad, worried; lips pressed tight together.

"You okay?"

"Yeah." His voice was soft, eyes flickering gently at my question.

"I'm sure they'll calm down in a minute. Have they argued like this before?"

"A couple times. Not too often."

"What's it usually about?"

Ryan sighed, "The same thing this one is about."

"What do you mean?"

"Mallory and other guys."

"They like each other, right? I noticed it that day at the mall."

"Yeah, that's been going on for a while now."

"What do you mean?" I asked, leaning forward on the table.

"They like each other, but they won't do anything about it."

"Why?"

Ryan stopped moving his hands and let them just rest in his lap, "Kevin won't be with her because of everything that's going on for him at home, with the money problems."

"Because he works so much?"

He nodded, "Yeah, he doesn't have time to really be the boy-friend that he thinks she deserves so he won't let himself do anything with her."

I looked up and out the window to where Mallory and Kevin were standing in the parking lot. Things seemed to have calmed down now. They were still talking, but their bodies were less rigid, arms hanging loosely at their sides.

"How do you know that?"

"He told me."

"Does she know that's why he won't be with her?"

"I think so."

I could see Ryan's body begin to relax as we talked. He leaned back in his chair, hands clasped together between his knees. His eyes had stopped moving over the chess pieces and were now resting on his hands. I hoped this was a sign that he was warming up to me, getting more comfortable. There was something that happened when I was with him, something I couldn't quite place, that made me want him to like me, need him to like me. I wanted him to feel safe with me, the kind of safety that he felt with Mallory and Kevin, but maybe more than that. Maybe something more than just feeling safe.

"So why do you think she's talking about this other guy like that in front of him? It seems a little mean, like she's throwing it in his face."

Ryan was quiet for a moment. "I don't know. I don't know why she's doing it."

Part of me still wanted to reach over and take his hand, run my fingers across the skin on the top, let his discomfort find relief in me. I stayed still. We weren't there yet.

Mallory and Kevin came back in and sat down in their seats. They didn't look at each other directly or even speak to one another. Kevin took a breath and made a move on the board.

"Your turn." His voice sounded tired, but I could tell he was making an attempt at normalcy, trying to act like everything was fine now and hadn't gotten as heated as it had been five minutes prior.

I watched as Ryan made a move, his eyes going from the piece in his hand to Kevin and then Mallory. They seemed okay now. It didn't seem like anything had been resolved, but it appeared that everything would be okay and stay that way for at least a while.

Mallory looked up at me, "Wanna get coffee with me?" She raised her eyebrows just enough to let me know that she wanted to talk with me privately.

"Yeah, sure."

We stood up and headed for the front counter. There was no line, the barista leaning back against one of the espresso machines, book in hand. Mallory placed her order and we stepped over to the hand off area.

She glanced over at the table before looking up at me, "I'm sorry about that. Is Ryan okay? I don't want to upset him, especially now."

"Yeah, I think he'll be fine. He said you guys have argued before."

She looked down at her feet, "Kevin means well, he's not actually angry at me."

I looked back over at the table. Kevin's shoulders were looser as he bent over the board again, attempting to strategize a move. Ryan looked up at Mallory and me and she smiled at him. Mallory got her drink and we headed back over to the table. She and Kevin eventually started talking again, debating the level of reality in some movie. For the remainder of the night, Kevin's left arm and Mallory's right hand stayed inches apart from each other on the table, never moving closer, never touching.

My parents fighting began to get worse. Over the next couple weeks, they started to argue more and more frequently. I would come home from school or from hanging out with my friends and find them in their bedroom fussing at each other again. Sometimes it would go for a long time. I would be in bed, trying to go to sleep, and I could hear their voices through the wall, muffled and yet still so sharp.

I spent a lot of time wondering about Brooke. What had her time in this room been like? What had she struggled with that had led her to write those things on the wall? It seemed like whatever it was had been pretty bad. One of her writings said,

I don't know how much more of this I can take

Had it been something at school? Was she bullied like Ryan? Or was she like me? Did her parents fight, too?

It was exhausting being at home sometimes, hearing them go at it the way they did. I began finding any reason I could to get out of the house on days when they were going to be home together for a long period of time. Fortunately, I could just go see my friends.

I met Theo the weekend before Thanksgiving break. It was a Sunday night and Kevin was working. Mallory had texted me asking if we could all hang out so I could meet him. She wanted me to meet him before Kevin so I could help her gauge whether or not he and Kevin would get along.

We met at the Burger King on Lancaster Street. I got there minutes before they did and sat down at a table in the corner. When they arrived, with Ryan in tow, I waved them over.

Theo was tall, quite a bit taller than Mallory, and well-muscled with big arms and a broad chest. His blonde hair was short and combed. His t-shirt wasn't wrinkled and his jeans didn't have any holes or rips.

Mallory looked at me as I shook Theo's hand.

"It's nice to meet you, man." Theo said, his voice deep. "Mallory's told me a lot about you guys. She said you're the new member of the pack."

I nodded, "Yeah, I guess that'd be right."

"She said you're a writer? Or is that you, Ryan?" he looked at Mallory for confirmation.

"That's me. I don't know if I'm a writer, but I like to do it." I said, feeling shy. I never referred to myself directly as a writer. I always felt like I couldn't do that until I had gotten published.

"If you write, you're a writer," Theo replied. "I always wished I could do something like that. I've never been much in the arts department. You and Mallory have me beat with the writing and photography."

"Everybody has some kind of talent. Yours just isn't in the arts, that's all." Mallory said, punching him in the shoulder lightly and smiling when he turned to her.

"Yeah," I said. "And besides, you're going into the Marines, right? That's really impressive. I mean, I wouldn't be able to do that. I'm not strong enough." I tried to flex my bicep and we all laughed when nothing happened. Ryan put an elbow up on the table, leaning into his palm. I looked at him and winked.

"Oh, anybody can get physically strong. You could even come work out with me if you want some help getting bigger. The hard part is the mental. It's the determination and the commitment and learning to trust both your own choices and your brothers. People get it mixed up all the time, thinking it's all physical, but the mental aspect is what's hard."

"I guess you're right. I never really thought about it that way." I replied.

Theo turned and looked around, "Where's the restroom?"

"I think it's around that corner," Mallory pointed to a little hallway beside the registers. Theo got up and headed over there. As soon as he was gone, Mallory turned to Ryan and me and leaned in close.

"All right, what's the verdict? Is he okay?" Her face was serious, like she was asking for advice on some major life-altering dilemma.

"He seems really cool," I said.

"Yeah," Ryan nodded. "He's really nice."

"But what else?" She said, holding her hands. "Do you think it'll be okay when he meets Kevin? I mean, Kevin's not an asshole or anything, but I know he's not exactly a fan of the whole *leaving for the Marines in April* situation, so I don't want there to be any more tension than there's already going to be."

"I mean, I think it'll be fine, but . . ." I wasn't sure how to say what I wanted to say.

Mallory looked worried, "What? What is it?"

"I just . . ." I looked at Ryan, wondering if he was thinking the same thing I was. "Why is it so important for Kevin to meet him? I think you know how Kevin's going to feel if you have them meet and I don't understand why you want him to feel like that. His feelings aren't your problem, but still."

She was quiet for a minute, eyes on the table. "I don't *want* him to feel like that. There's more to it than that." She sighed and ran her fingers through her hair, dark strands sliding across her forehead.

"Then explain it to me because I don't understand."

"I really do love him, but I can't just wait around for him. He's never gonna give himself a break. I don't want to hurt him, but I have to live my life. Theo's a really good guy. He may be leaving in April, but I really like spending time with him."

"But you might get hurt when he leaves." Ryan added, looking over at her through worried eyes.

"No, I won't. I'm not going to get attached to him. He already told me himself that he doesn't want to hurt me when he leaves so we should just keep things simple. We're both being smart about this. I'm being smart."

His eyes lingered on her for a moment more before looking at mine. His mouth was tight and his eyebrows were tense. I had been around him long enough now to tell when he was worried about something. I smiled at him. He gave me a slow nod.

Theo came back from the restroom and sat down. We talked for another hour, going from Theo's army training to movies while eating large orders of fries. Every now and then, I saw Ryan look over at Mallory, that same worried look on his face.

Mallory was the kind of person who always seemed to be thinking things through, making the smart decision. Despite that, part of me felt like this wasn't something she'd fully thought through. She seemed really happy with Theo and he was a really cool guy, but there was still the fact that he was leaving in five months. What would she do then? I worried that, despite what they said, they wouldn't be able to keep things simple for five whole months. There was no way for them to know how close they would get in those five months and how they would feel when the time came for him to leave in April.

"Don't worry," I said to Ryan quietly as we all got up to leave later in the evening. "She'll be okay."

He nodded and we all left, Theo shaking my hand again as they went to get in Mallory's car. As I drove home, I wondered if they really would be okay. I wondered if Mallory had thought things through or if, for once, she was finally giving herself a break from thinking.

My grandmother came for Thanksgiving. She arrived Wednesday night from Indianapolis and took up a spot in our guest room. We alternated Thanksgivings with my mom and my father's families and this year it was my mom's turn. My mom was an only child and my grandfather had died years ago, so my grandmother was the only one to come.

Her name was Evelyn Carmichael and she looked exactly like my mother. They had the same kind eyes and happy smile. Even more alike was their hair. They both had the same bright red hair, long and flowing around their shoulders. My grandma was very thin without seeming frail. She was still very active, always telling us about her friend, Linda, who she walked with every day. Linda was apparently several years younger than my grandma and ran 5k's. They would go on a five mile walk every day and talk about Linda's boyfriends. Currently, Linda was dating a car salesman who would take her for rides in the Maserati.

"Well, hello, my grandson!" she said as she walked into the kitchen after settling in upstairs.

I was doing homework at the kitchen table while Mom cooked dinner. The kitchen was filling with the smell of roasted asparagus and turkey burgers. The light outside was slowly fading, the lamp in the corner behind me becoming brighter. My grandmother came and sat down across from me at the table.

"Is that homework? What subject?"

"Biology," I said with a sigh.

"Weighing you down? I hated Biology. Worst subject I ever studied. Now, history . . . that was my specialty. I could tell you every date of every war and major event in the book. You know, I almost became a history teacher when I was in college. I was studying social work at the University of Michigan and I almost switched majors so I could become a history teacher. I even made an appointment with my advisor, but I didn't end up going." Her hands smoothed over the placemat as she spoke, an action I had seen my mother do many times in my life.

"What made you decide to stay with social work?" I asked, setting my pencil down on the table by my notebook.

"Well, there was a little girl that lived in the same apartment building as me, just one floor down. I used to see her playing on the sidewalk when I would come back from class." Her eyes seemed to be lost somewhere, deep in the memory of her story. "One day I came home to find her sitting on the steps with a police officer. There were several cop cars outside the building. Her parents were getting put into two of them. It turned out they had been making her sleep in the bathtub every night because they were packaging cocaine in what had been her bedroom. They were making that poor girl live the bathroom, sleeping in a cold tub every night. I saw that and I knew that I had to finish my degree so I could help kids like that. It's a nasty world out there, grandson, and you must do all you can to make it better. Otherwise, what are you doing with your life?"

I looked over at my mom who had stopped cooking during my grandmother's story. She was just leaning against the counter, a glass of water in her hand, listening. My grandmother had that kind of effect on a room. People listened to her when she spoke.

There was a soft rumble as my father's car pulled into the driveway. A few moments later, the door opened and he stepped into the kitchen. His work uniform was wrinkled as he shut the door behind him and turned to see grandma. My mother turned back to the stove.

"Hello there, stranger." My grandma stood and held her arms open, taking him in a big hug. Letting go, she stepped back with one hand on each of his arms and looked up into his face. "I see you're still sporting that mess on your face." My grandma didn't approve of facial hair.

My father gave her a small smile before stepping around to the sink to wash his hands. "How are you, Mrs. Carmichael?"

"Oh, I'm fine, I'm fine. How are *you*, Saul? Work treating you well?"

My father dried his hands on a towel and removed his keys from his pocket and tossed them into the junk drawer by the stove along with his wallet. "Yes, ma'am, I'm still dragging along. I'm gonna go take a shower real quick. How long till dinner?" He turned to my mother.

"Twenty minutes," she said, not looking at him, her eyes back on her cooking.

"All right," He replied, walking out of the kitchen.

My grandma looked at my mother, "Do you want some help, Melanie?"

"No, Mom. I've got it. You just relax and spend time with Peter." Her voice was quieter than it had been for most of the afternoon since Grandma had gotten there. She had been talking non-stop since she'd arrived. I could see her arm slowly moving in circles, stirring the gravy for the potatoes she was making.

"Everything all right, dear?"

"Yep, I'm just trying to get dinner ready." This was what my father being home did to my mom. It made her quiet and withdrawn.

My grandmother turned to me and smiled, raising her eyebrows. She wasn't blind.

The Thanksgiving meal was nice. My mom made her delicious sweet potato casserole, and my father made his family's bean dip before spending the rest of the morning in the living room watching the Macy's parade. Grandma took care of the turkey, a task she wouldn't let anyone assist her with. I helped with the green beans and the fruit salad.

As we ate, we all sat around the kitchen table and talked about what we were thankful for.

"I'm thankful for my family," my grandma said, looking at each of us.

"I'm thankful that I have such a kind, responsible son." My mother smiled at me.

My father was quiet before saying, "I'm thankful for the roof over our heads and the food on our table." My mother looked down at her plate as he spoke, and I wondered if she had been hoping he would say her or our family.

Not wanting to repeat family, I said, "I'm thankful for all the ways God has blessed me this year."

We ate and had seconds and thirds and then sliced up grandma's pumpkin pie. I looked at my mother and my father and the fact that they weren't talking directly to one another, most of the conversation revolving around my grandmother. And that was when I realized what I was really thankful for: my grandmother, who was keeping things calm between my parents, even if it was just for a little while.

And just like that Christmas was upon us. The day after Thanksgiving, radio stations began playing songs of cheer and eggnog, of holiday romance and little mangers in Bethlehem. All my neighbors started lugging cardboard boxes full of garland and twinkle lights into their front yards, bushes and trees being lit by nightfall in a bright, white glow. Down the street, the Basset's son, Edward, spent most of that Saturday on a ladder in the front yard lifting strands of lights above his head to hook to the roof. Mrs. Basset sat in a lawn chair positioned in the dying grass so she could see everything without having to crane her neck. A maroon blanket rested around her shoulders as her knitting needles moved busily in front of her. Mr. Basset didn't rest. He spent the entire afternoon holding the ladder, giving instructions, or trying to get on the roof himself. Edward could be heard yelling at him from down the street.

"Dad, stop! Dad, you're not middle aged anymore!"

I spent most of the afternoon on our front steps, the outside of our house devoid of any Christmas cheer, watching the whole street in action. My notebook rested in my lap. Only a few sentences had made it onto the page during the hour I'd been out there. I'd become so distracted by the people-watching that I'd forgotten that I'd even brought it outside with me.

The single mother who lived across the street from us was trying to fix the red ribbon on her Christmas wreath that was hanging on her front door. Her two small children, who each looked to be no older than five, were in a stroller next to the door. Their crying and wailing echoed through the street. After several unsuccessful attempts with the ribbon, she finally ripped the bow off. She stared at the box-less wreath for a moment before shrugging and moving on to putting lights in the flowerbed. The children continued to cry, but she somehow didn't let it get to her. Every few moments, she would lean down to kiss the top of each child's head.

At the house to her left there was a family of four working in the front yard. The parents were wrapping lights around the bushes that grew in front of the bay window. Closer to the middle of the yard their teenage kids, a boy and girl set of twins, were trying to set up an inflatable nativity scene. The boy, blond and clad in a rather ugly Christmas sweater, was having trouble starting the electric box that was attached to where the back of the stable would be. His sister, also blonde, stood behind him and pointed down at something on the box. A moment later, air started filling the nativity, Mary and Joseph standing tall over their little baby Jesus. The twins high-fived and stood to the side smiling as they watched the result of their work.

Behind me, the front door opened and closed. The soft patter of my grandmother's slippers stepped across the porch and down the steps to sit next to me. She had a black, wool shawl wrapped around her body, her red hair hanging loose over her shoulder. It was so vibrant in contrast to the black. It reminded me of my mother's and the way it would spread out across her white, cotton pillowcase as she would read books to me on Saturday mornings when I was little. It seemed almost muted now, like a light had been shining through it at one point, but not anymore.

"It's nice out here," my grandmother said, running her hands up and down her shins. "It gets so hot in that house sometimes."

"What's going on in there?"

"Oh, your dad's just putting up the tree. Your mother's getting something in the oven for dinner."

I looked over at her, following her eyes as she scanned the same houses I had been watching moments earlier, "Are they talking?"

"No," she said. "They're not."

She understood. Even though she didn't say anything, had never said anything to me about it, I knew she understood. It was in her voice, thick with age and history, full of a motherly wisdom that had grown as she'd gotten older. She brought her hands to her lap and clasped them tightly together, rubbing her thumbs against the wrinkled skin that covered her knuckles. Even though she had never talked to me about the situation with my parents, I knew that she would if I needed her to. There was this unspoken bond between us, one that I could feel during times like this that assured me that if I needed to talk, she would be there. I was also certain that she would know when that time came before I did.

She looked over at me and down at the notebook in my lap, "You're still writing, I see."

I picked up my notebook, running my hand across the purple cover, "I haven't really written anything since I came out here, but yeah."

"Good, you've always been a wonderful writer," she smiled. "It always seemed to make you happy."

"It does," I smiled back.

She was silent for a moment then, "I hope there are other things in your life that make you happy too."

I looked over to see her watching me. Her eyes were soft as they looked into mine.

"Yeah, I have some good friends."

"I'm glad."

She sighed loudly and stood up, a soft shudder in her breath as she straightened out her legs.

"All right, Grandson. Let's fill this house with some Christmas cheer."

I stood and followed her inside, the sound of Edward Basset scolding his father fading away as we shut the door behind us.

We spent the rest of the afternoon decorating. It took my father another hour to get our tree up and thirty minutes more to get the lights to work. Afterwards, he was so tired and frustrated that he went to bed early. I finished setting up our advent calendar on the table in the foyer right as my mom was pulling dinner out of the oven.

I loved when my grandma was over for dinner. Partly because she always had the best stories. It never failed that we would talk about something that would remind her of some moment or event or person. She would get so wrapped up in her stories, too. Most of the time she would change her voice with the different people and use really dramatic gestures. It would always have my mom laughing. That was another reason why it was great having her over. Anytime Mom was smiling was good.

After dinner, I got a text:

Mallory: *I'm coming to pick you up. Be available.*

Ryan was in the passenger seat when I climbed in the back. He turned and smiled as I buckled up. Mallory was behind the wheel, her hands tapping out the beat to a Christmas song that was playing on the radio.

"Where's Kevin?" I asked as she pulled out of my driveway and headed down the street.

"He's working tonight which works out well for us because Santa is gonna come early this year." I could see her smiling in the rearview mirror.

"What does that mean?"

"Well, dear Peter, it means that *we* are going to play the role of Santa's little elves and bring some Christmas joy to the Johnson household. When they moved out of their old house, they had to get rid of a lot of stuff since they wouldn't have as much space in the apartment. They chose to keep some other stuff that their parents owned instead of all their Christmas decorations. Last Christmas they didn't put up *anything*. They said they were glad that they kept what they did, but, come on, it kinda sucks to not have any decorations to put up. So that is where Head-Elf Diaz and her comrades come in! We're gonna go pick up a bunch of Christmas decorations from Walgreens and take them over to his house and put them up before he gets home."

"Is Jeremy gonna be okay with that?"

"We'll find out," she replied, once again smiling into the rear-view mirror.

I smiled back and turned to Ryan. He was staring straight ahead watching the road. From the side, I could see the light from the town shining in his eyes.

"Hey."

He turned when I spoke, his eyes meeting mine for only a second before falling to some other point on my face.

"Hi."

"How was your Thanksgiving?"

"It was nice. How was yours?"

"It was okay. Not the most memorable."

His eyes went back up to mine for a moment, just looking, almost like he was reading words in them. Then, "I'm sorry."

There was something in the way he said it that made me feel like he knew, could somehow see in my eyes what I was going through with my parents. He couldn't have known what was going on, obviously, but there was something that made me feel like he did or at least understood that I wasn't being upfront about the stuff at home.

I tried to smile, "It's all fine. Thanks though."

He looked at me for a moment longer before turning back around in his seat.

We drove in silence for a few seconds before Mallory spoke again.

"So does anybody care about how my Thanksgiving was?"

Mallory had already made a list of everything we would be getting, so as soon as we stepped into Walgreens we got to work. Thirty minutes later, we reconvened in the photo department to examine our finds. Mallory had found a three-foot Christmas tree that she said would fit nicely on the coffee table in their den. She also had three packs of lights that would change colors when hooked up and a children's wooden Nativity. On my end I had been able to find a couple boxes of red and silver ball ornaments as well as a box that had ornaments that were a mixture of stars, snowflakes, and Santa figurines. For the top of the tree, I had found a silver-colored plastic star. Ryan had found some garland which he brought to us in his arms like a snake, coiled around his elbows. Mallory paid for everything when we checked out. She said she'd been saving for this.

"How's Theo?" I asked as we pulled out of the parking lot and headed for Kevin and Jeremy's apartment.

"He's good. His grandparents live in Fort Wayne, so they all went there for Thanksgiving. I talked to him earlier and he said they'd had a good time."

When we pulled into a parking space outside Kevin's building, we grabbed our bags and headed upstairs.

Jeremy was holding a dish towel when he opened the door. His eyes went straight to the bags in our arms.

"Wha- "

"Merry Christmas!" we called out before pushing inside and getting to work.

Kevin didn't say anything at first. When he opened the door, we were in the den next to the tree. We had it set up on the coffee table. The star I'd found had ended up being a little too heavy for the tree, so the top leaned slightly. The nativity had replaced the flower vase on the end table next to the couch. We had wrapped the garland around the door frame to the kitchen along with a strand of lights we had left over.

The four of us stood there watching Kevin, Jeremy standing in the doorway to the kitchen. Kevin just stood there for a moment, his eyes moving up the Christmas tree. He looked over at Jeremy.

"Look what they did for ya, Kev."

"We did it for *both* of you." Mallory spoke up, smiling at Jeremy and then at Kevin. "You both deserve a merry Christmas."

She skipped over to where Jeremy was standing and flipped off the light switch on the wall. It was when my eyes finally adjusted to the lights from the tree, illuminating the dark room, that I realized Kevin was crying. His wet eyes sparkled as the light on his face faded from green to red to gold. No sounds or words came from his mouth. The light in his eyes said everything. Kevin, who cared for and looked after everyone, needed to be taken care of and looked after too. Mallory had made sure we were there for that, for him. That was what this was all about. It wasn't about decorating or helping make their Christmas better. It was about showing Kevin that we were there, that he was being taken care of too.

Jeremy stepped forward and placed a hand on Kevin's shoulder. This woke Kevin from his daze and he looked up at his brother.

For the first time since Mallory had explained everything in the car that evening, I realized something. The last time Kevin and Jeremy had decorated for Christmas was also their last Christmas with their parents. My chest felt tight at the thought of the memories this was probably bringing up for them. Mallory must have known this when she thought up her plan. She must have known, but also somehow guessed that they wouldn't be angry. They weren't. Despite the tears, Kevin was happy. Maybe he was welcoming the memories. Maybe, somewhere deep in his mind, he was with them again.

"You okay, brother?" Jeremy said as he looked at Kevin.

"I-" his lips fluttered open gently, "I . . ."

His eyes moved from Jeremy's and turned towards Mallory. In two quick steps he had his arms around her.

"Thank you," he breathed. Releasing her, he stepped over to Ryan and me, still standing next to the tree. He threw one arm over each of our shoulders and pulled us into a double hug.

"Thank you."

When he let go, he turned to the tree once more, "It's beautiful."

"It really is," Jeremy said, running the dish cloth he'd been holding through his hands. "Now, you guys go wash up. The three of you are staying for ice cream."

He stepped back into the kitchen, but not before catching Mallory's eye and giving her a nod. I sat down on the couch, Ryan sitting next to me. Mallory stayed by the wall and the three of us watched Kevin. He lifted his hand and slid his fingers between the bristles along the tree limbs.

I watched him and thought of all the working, all the studying, all the worrying for everyone else throughout the day, every day, always with a smile on his lips. I thought, *I want you to be happy, Kevin. I truly, truly want you to be happy. You deserve that much.*

"My stomach hurts."

We were in my room and Mallory was laying across my bed, hands rubbing her stomach as if she were pregnant. I was sitting at my desk, looking over some pages I'd written the night before while my parents were arguing. Ryan sat at the end of my bed, doodling in his notebook.

"You know," I said, turning in my chair to look at Mallory. "You didn't have to eat the extra slice of garlic bread."

"What?" She leaned up on her elbows, "One does not leave a slice of garlic bread to be tossed away into the garbage."

"I don't think my mom was going to throw it away."

"Still!" She rolled her eyes and laid back down, resuming rubbing circles into her stomach.

We were waiting for Kevin to get there. He was working the evening shift and was supposed to get off at eight.

I had spent most of the afternoon working on college applications. I had applied to various schools in Indiana and Illinois, as well as one in Wisconsin. On most of the applications, I had put "undecided" for my major. The only time I didn't do that was when I was filling out an application for an art school in Chicago that had a creative writing department. It seemed naive to study writing, but, frankly, I just wanted to see if I would get in.

I didn't like the idea of going too far away. Lately, I'd been thinking about what it would be like for my parents when I left for college. I knew they'd continue to fight like they always did, but what about my mom? What would she do? For a long time, it felt like I had been a kind of distraction from everything that was going on with my father. We would play games or watch a movie after their fights, and she would perk up a bit. It always made her feel better when we would do something fun like that after something happened with my father. What would she do if I left? Would she watch movies by herself? I didn't like to think about it, but I felt like I had to. I didn't want her to become depressed if I left, if I wasn't there to help cheer her up. What would happen then?

After thinking about that all day, I needed a distraction. I texted the group and asked if they wanted to come over for dinner. So there we were, Mallory holding her stomach and Ryan drawing at the end of my bed.

I watched Ryan, his pencil scribbling across the page. He didn't look at me, his head turned down to the notebook, but I could see his teeth come out to bite his bottom lip. There was something beautiful about the way he looked when he was concentrating. Maybe it was his eyelashes, the way they fluttered slightly. Or the way he would lean his head down and a bit of hair would fall into his face. He would lift a hand and brush it back, the soft strands sliding between his fingers.

"Hey," Mallory said from the bed, and I looked up to see Kevin standing at the door. He had on his black work jeans and polo, clothes he had told me once were appropriately uncomfortable for work. His black curls were a little messy as he untucked his shirt from his jeans and plopped down on the bed between Mallory and Ryan, his head coming to rest in his palm.

"Sorry I'm late," he said, turning on his side, a sigh falling from his lips. "I had to talk to my boss about the schedule for next week."

"Everything okay?" I asked.

"Yeah, I just wanted to try to pick up an extra shift or two." he replied. "Is Theo coming tonight?"

"Nope," Mallory said, looking down at him. "He's hanging out with his family tonight."

As she said this, I could see Kevin's body relaxing a bit. I'm sure Mallory could see it too. His entire body seemed to sink down into the bed a little more.

"Well . . . you should bring him around. We should all hang out."

I could see on Kevin's face that he didn't mean the words. Not in a mean way, but not genuine either. His face was blank as he spoke. I was sure Mallory couldn't see his face from her angle above him, but she had to know that he was just saying them to be a good friend. She had been right when she said that she had to live her life and not let this thing with Kevin hold her back, but I knew she still was concerned that it would hurt him when he finally saw them together. It would hurt him, and I hated to see it too, but maybe she was right. If Kevin wasn't going to allow himself to be with her in that way, she couldn't just sit around and wait for him. I don't think he expected her to, but there was no way of avoiding the pain that would undoubtedly come when she finally brought Theo around.

"How was work?" I asked, trying to move the conversation away from Mallory and Theo.

Kevin reached across Mallory and grabbed a pillow to put under his head, "It was okay. I was up late last night doing homework, so I'm just tired." He looked at Ryan. "What about you? Today been okay?"

Ryan nodded, "Yeah, yeah, I'm okay."

"You sure?"

"Yep, I'm fine. I promise." He gave a little nod to Kevin before turning back to the notebook.

Ryan seemed to have been okay the past few weeks. Though he had been quiet for a while, he had slowly started to open up. He had certainly opened up with me. His body language wasn't as nervous or shy around me as it had once been. He seemed to be much more comfortable now, even more comfortable than when I had first met him. He was healing.

Kevin watched him for another moment or two before closing his eyes. He and Mallory had both been there to help Ryan get better the first time he had tried to OD. I wondered what they saw when they looked at him. Was that all they could see? Ryan in a hospital bed? I wondered if they were both constantly worrying about him. After going through that twice, would he try to do it again? He had promised Kevin he wouldn't, but was that something you could promise? He had been hurting so badly when he did it. If he felt that kind of pain again, he might not even think about the promise he made. He might just look for the relief.

He was so beautiful sitting there on the bed. I wanted to clear his mind of all the things that worried him. There was obviously so much on his mind that he had to deal with. I just wanted to make it all go away so he could be happy. He deserved to be happy, to be free of all that pain. I had never met someone like him who was dealing with that much. I had no idea how to relieve him of it.

After a little bit, I got up to go to the bathroom. When I came back, I stopped just outside my door. Kevin and Mallory were still laying across my bed. Kevin's eyes were closed, asleep. Mallory was looking down at him, his head next to hers, her eyes on the side of his face. Her hand was resting at the top of his head and her fingers were brushing through the black curls that were hanging down over his forehead. The corners of her mouth were turned up slightly. I wondered what it was like for her, being in love with someone who was holding himself back from her. She loved him, I could see it in her eyes, in her movements, as she sat there running her fingers across his forehead. What did it feel like to want someone who wanted you, but wouldn't let themselves have you? It made me wonder about her relationship with Theo. Was that the whole point of being with him? If she couldn't be with Kevin, was Theo an okay replacement? Did she really feel something with Theo or was she just trying to find someone to give that love to?

I walked back to my desk and, as I did, Mallory saw me and let her hand fall beside her. I looked at her and smiled. She turned away as if nothing had happened. The three of us continued to talk about school or jokes or anything that came up while Kevin lay next to Mallory, sleeping peacefully away.

13

"Peter, these pages are *really* good."

Mrs. Stroud and I were standing in the parking lot after school. I had given her some more work on Wednesday, the chapter just before the end, and she was returning them with her notes.

"I feel like you're really making progress towards that ending. How are you feeling about it?" A strand of her short black hair was fluttering around in the wind next to her face.

I shrugged, "I don't know. I mean, I'm still having trouble mapping it out. I tried to work on it last night, but I just got frustrated. I keep coming back to Connor going to get her."

"Well, Peter, this is *your* story. If that's the ending you feel confident about than write it. I just think you should give it a little more time. It's *so* close."

I looked across the mostly empty parking lot. It was the last day before Christmas break. I was excited about not having to get up early for school for two weeks, but the thought of being at home all the time, listening to my parents fight, left an uneasy feeling in my stomach.

"I haven't seen your dad at church the past few weeks. Has he been working a lot?" I turned back to her, her eyes squinting in the sunlight to look at me.

"Yeah, he is." It was easier to lie than to tell her that he wasn't there because my parents were always arguing late into the night, and he'd still be asleep on the couch when we got up to leave in the morning.

I wasn't going to tell her about my parents. Mrs. Stroud was one of the few adults in my life that I felt like I could confide in and talk to. She'd helped me so much over the past year. I'd spent so much time talking to her about my struggles with writing and how I felt like nothing I wrote was good enough. Every time I'd told her about some insecurity I was feeling, she'd always been able to help.

Part of the reason why I didn't tell her was because it felt like airing dirty laundry. It seemed odd to tell someone about all the trouble my parents were having. I hadn't even told my friends. It almost seemed like a secret I wasn't supposed to tell anyone, and if I did it would be a betrayal to my parents.

The other part of it was that Mrs. Stroud was the only person in my life who seemed genuinely happy. Everyone else around me was struggling with something. Kevin had his money problems and his non-relationship with Mallory; Mallory had college and Theo; Ryan had his own set of struggles; my parents had each other. Everyone had something except for Mrs. Stroud. She was the only person I could talk to and not think about what they were going through themselves, what pain *they* might be dealing with. I could just talk to her about my writing and her family and church. There wasn't any heaviness to our discussions. I didn't want to bring my personal problems into that. I didn't want to ruin it.

Our Christmas was quiet. We didn't get up early on Christmas morning, just slept late and opened presents after we had breakfast. All sitting around the tree in the living room, we took turns opening gifts. My mom gave my father a new plaid button down that he smiled at and said he liked. He gave her a book she'd mentioned as well as some more of her favorite perfume. I had gotten my mother a set of nice candles and my father a framed picture of our family to put on his desk at work. As I watched him open it, I realized that it was a strange gift considering how things had been lately. He said he couldn't wait to put it in his office. I got cash and some new clothes and books and then we sat around watching *A Christmas Story* on TBS.

It was a fine Christmas, but it felt strange. It was like all the tension that had taken over our house the past several months had dissipated long enough for us to enjoy the holiday together.

14

For New Year's Eve, we decided to "stick our middle fingers up to the holiday" (Mallory's words). The Empty Cup was staying open till 1 a.m. as a safe alternative to a night out drinking. We decided we would ring in the new year over mugs of hot chocolate instead of glasses of champagne.

Mallory made it known in advance that Theo would be coming as a way of giving a heads up to Kevin. He hadn't been with us whenever she brought him along, so this would be their first-time meeting.

My mom was planning on sleeping her way into the new year. When I left the house at 9, she was setting things out for her lunch in the morning. My father wouldn't be home from work for another hour.

"Are you sure you don't want me to stay?" I asked. "I could just tell them to come over here."

"Oh, I'll be fine. I'm just gonna go to bed. You go have fun with your friends." She replied, smiling. She had already put on her lavender nightgown and slippers. Her hair was pulled back from her face as she pulled a plastic salad bowl and lid out of the kitchen cabinet.

"Okay, I'll be back around 1, probably."

I left her standing in the kitchen, a soft humming coming from her lips as I shut the door behind me.

When I got to The Empty Cup, Mallory, Theo, and Ryan were already there. They were sitting around a table in the corner, next to one of the couches. As I walked over to them, I noticed that only one other table was occupied. It was taken by an elderly couple that reminded me of the Bassets. They both had their canes hooked on the back of their chairs as they talked quietly. The woman had dark hair and a bright blue sweater over her shoulders. Her date was a man with salt and pepper hair that was almost completely covered by his fedora. His brown cardigan looked a tad too small on his thin body. Their hands were joined in the middle of the table, his fingers holding hers in a gentle grasp.

Ryan was the first to look up when I walked over, his hand lifting in a small wave. Mallory and Theo both turned to see me.

"Hiya, friend" Mallory said, winking.

"Hey, man. How's it goin'?" Theo lifted his fist to bump against mine. His blonde hair was combed to the side, his Polo shirt unbuttoned at the top as he leaned back in his chair with one arm slung casually across the back of Mallory's.

I sat down, "Pretty good, when did you guys get here?"

"Like ten minutes ago," Mallory replied. "Kevin's on his way." She locked eyes with me for a moment. I could see how nervous she was as she leaned back into Theo's arm, his hand coming up to rub slowly against her right arm. Her body looked stiff. Theo turned to her.

"You okay, babe?"

"Yep, I'm fine." She replied, bringing her left hand up to pat his chest.

Theo looked at me, "I'm excited to finally meet the famous Kevin. You guys talk about him so much."

"He should be here soon." Mallory said, looking at me once more.

I didn't expect Kevin to be rude to Theo and I wasn't sure if Mallory did either. Kevin was too mature for that. The biggest concern for me was whether he would be hurt when he saw them together. Mallory had told me that Theo was the closest thing to a boyfriend she'd ever had (even though she refused to refer to him as her boyfriend). That meant this was the first time Kevin was having to deal with seeing her with another guy. I wondered what that would be like for him. He spent so much time trying to resist being with her. I couldn't imagine what it would feel like to see her with someone else.

"So, what have you guys been doing today?" I asked.

"I basically spent all afternoon writing this essay for a college application that I didn't decide to do until now." Mallory replied. "It's probably past the deadline, but I have all my other ones to fall back on just in case."

"Where is it?"

"University of Southern California. They have a great physical therapy program. I wasn't sure I wanted to go that far away, but they're one of the best programs in the country so it'd be stupid for me to not at least see if I can get in."

Ryan frowned. I couldn't tell if it was because of how far away the school was or because she wasn't going for photography. It made me sad, too, to think about her being stuck in school for years, doing something she didn't fully love. I understood her reasoning behind it, she was just trying to make the smart choice, but it sucked that the smart choice involved turning away from her passion.

"Did you get all yours done?" She asked.

"Yeah, I finished a couple weeks ago." I thought back to those few weeks, filling out applications with an "Undecided" major. While Mallory was going to school for something she didn't want to do, I was going with no idea *what* to do. I thought I would have it figured out by now.

It was at that point that I saw the door open behind Mallory and Theo. Kevin walked in. I watched him scan the room for us, his face falling when he finally saw us. He looked at me and I could see him straightening his back and his shoulders rise and fall with a sigh. He headed over to us.

Mallory was looking at me and turned as Kevin got to the table, "Hey, Kevin!" Her greeting was a tad over-excited. She immediately sat up and away from Theo's arm. He seemed to notice, sitting up straight next to her.

"Hey, guys." He replied, pulling up a chair between Ryan and me and sitting down.

Theo reached an arm across the table towards Kevin, "It's nice to meet you, man. I'm Theo."

"Kevin," he replied, taking Theo's hand and shaking it. I could see the muscles in Kevin's hand tighten just a bit as they shook. Theo's stayed relaxed.

"It's nice to finally meet you. I've heard a lot about you from these guys."

"Likewise," Kevin brought his hands down to his lap and I could see them join, his thumbs twirling.

"How was work?" Mallory asked, looking at Kevin as she took a sip of her coffee.

"Pretty slow. Nothing too exciting." Kevin was a subdued version of himself. His back was straight in his chair, his arms close to his body. He looked guarded, uncomfortable.

"You work at the mall, right? At Foot Locker?" Theo asked.

"Yep"

"That must suck, man."

Kevin's eyes met Theo's, a defensive edge going into his voice, "I do what I have to do to help out at home."

Theo's eyes got big for a moment, "Oh no, man! I didn't mean anything bad by it. I just meant it must suck to work in such a busy place. Whenever I go in there, there's always a ton of people around."

"Yeah," I chimed in, trying to save the conversation. "You guys get a lot of business. It must be hell sometimes."

Kevin settled back in his chair, "Yeah, I guess it does."

"So, Theo, how did you decide to join the Marines?" I asked, trying to change the subject.

He leaned forward on his elbows, "My grandfather was in the Marines when he was around my age. When I was younger, he used to tell me all these stories about that time in his life. It always seemed like less of a job and more of a duty that he felt he had. It was like being a Marine was what he was supposed to be all his life. He just seemed so sure of himself."

I could see Kevin out of the corner of my eye, lifting his head towards Theo, listening to what he was saying. Ryan sat quietly to my right.

"As I got older, I started to have that same feeling. Whenever I would look at my grandfather's photo albums or hear him re-tell some of those stories, I would get that feeling that he talked about. I started to feel like it was *my* duty too."

"Wow, that's really awesome." I replied. "My grandfather was in the Navy, but he died when I was really young, so I didn't get to hear any of his stories."

"It's pretty amazing stuff, man. You'd think it was all stories about being in combat, but a lot of what my grandfather told me was about stuff that happened between him and his Marine brothers. He told me about how being in the service bonds you to those other men in ways you wouldn't expect. Those bonds would carry over to when you were in action."

Theo had a smile on his face as he talked. It really seemed like the path he had chosen was one he was truly passionate about. I thought about what my path would be, if I could ever figure it out.

I turned to Kevin, who was sitting in his chair, his head turned toward Theo. His eyes seemed to be lost in space, hovering somewhere over the table. Ryan looked from Kevin to me.

I turned to him, "I think I need some hot chocolate. Wanna get some too, Ryan?"

He nodded and we both got up from the table and headed for the counter. We ordered two hot chocolates and went to stand over at the end where they would come out.

I turned to Ryan, "Do you think he's okay?"

"I don't know. He seems really sad."

"He has to know that she's not going to stay single forever, right? Like she said, she can't just wait around for him."

"Knowing that doesn't make it easier for him though."

I turned back to the table. Kevin was looking at Mallory and Theo again, his lips moving. He was talking. That was a good sign.

We got our drinks and went back to the table. Mallory and Kevin were talking about school, Theo chiming in occasionally with comments about his graduation the previous year. Kevin seemed to be looking mostly at Mallory as he spoke but would look over at Theo whenever he said something. He was loosening up a bit.

As Mallory talked, her hands moved under the table, her eyes falling to her lap every few seconds.

My phone vibrated:

Mallory: *Is this weird? I feel like it's weird.*

Me: *I think it's fine.*

Mallory: *But what about Kevin?*

Me: *Just give him time. He's gotta get used to it.*

Mallory looked up at me and sighed. Kevin was looking at Theo, who was talking about a teacher he'd had that was obsessed with Winnie the Pooh.

It would take time, but I was sure Kevin would come around. It was obviously a difficult situation. Kevin was smart though, and mature. He would do the right thing.

We sat there for the rest of the night talking, playing cards, and drinking hot chocolate and coffee. Kevin didn't talk as much as he normally did, but he remained polite. At midnight, we gave a collective roll of the eyes and got up to go. It was as anti-climactic as expected, but it was a nice night as we all walked out into the parking lot. Mallory and Theo got in his car, leaving Kevin, Ryan, and me alone.

"So was that okay?" I asked him as he opened his car door.

He sighed, "I don't know. I just . . . I don't know." He leaned his head down against the side of his car. "I just hate having to sit there and look at them . . . together. I know I have to. I know I have to grin and bear it, but it's just so friggin' hard." He turned his head to look at me and I could see the frustration in his eyes.

I wasn't sure what to say, what advice to give. I didn't know what words would ease his pain. Instead of speaking, I leaned forward and wrapped my arms around him. He leaned into the hug, placing his head against my shoulder. We stood there for a moment in the empty parking lot before parting.

"Thanks," he said, patting me on the arm. "I needed that. I'll see you guys later."

Ryan and I walked across the parking lot and got in my car. I had been driving him home a lot more lately. The past few times we'd all hung out, Ryan would look at me as we all got up to leave wherever we were and would just follow me to my car. It wasn't something that we ever talked about or acknowledged. The last time it had happened, a couple of days prior to New Year's, Mallory had winked at me as she got into Theo's car, looking from Ryan to me.

I liked driving Ryan home. I didn't know why, but those ten minutes in the car with him were oddly nice. Maybe it was because he'd really been opening up to me as a friend, talking more when we were together. Or maybe it was because he wanted to ride with me, to spend time with me away from everyone else.

"How was therapy this week?" I asked as we pulled out of the parking lot.

"It was okay. She says I've been more open to doing the work this time." Out of the corner of my eye I could see him looking out the window.

"Do you feel like you are?"

"I think so. I still feel bad sometimes, but . . . it's not as bad as before. And I want to keep it that way." His voice was quiet and slow, as if getting any louder might hurt him somehow.

"That's good." I wanted to look over at him, see how his face looked, how his eyes looked, as he spoke.

We were quiet for a moment.

"Do you mind if I ask you something?" I wasn't sure if I was allowed to ask this, if it would ruin what we had with our drive home.

"Sure."

"What do you mean when you say you feel bad?" I took a quick glance over at him as I paused at a stop sign. The glow from the streetlamp on the corner was illuminating his face as he stared down at his feet. His face was blank, giving me no indication as to whether I had crossed a line or not. I pulled away from the stop sign.

"I'm sorry. You don't have to answer that."

"No," he finally said. "It's fine. I . . . Sometimes I don't like myself very much."

"What do you mean? In what way?"

"Like . . . I don't know. I just feel like I'm not a real person, like who I am isn't important." His words came out slow, almost careful. I wanted to look at him again. "Sometimes I look in the mirror and hate what I see."

We were at his house. I pulled the car over to the curb and turned the ignition off. I turned in my seat to look at him. He was looking out the window at his house.

"Ryan."

He didn't look at me, but instead turned to gaze down at his shoes once more.

"I know that the stuff you deal with is really hard and I know that me saying this isn't going to suddenly make you feel better. But I just really want you to know that I think you're important and I think you're real and that you matter to me. I'm really glad that I've met you and that we're friends. We're friends, right?"

He nodded slowly, still not turning to me.

I continued, "And I think you're really beautiful. So when you look in the mirror, please remember that. Try to not hate what you see. I don't."

I stopped talking and waited. I didn't want to push him or make him uncomfortable, but I couldn't just let him get out of my car and go inside his house without saying something after he opened up to me like that. Had he told that stuff to Mallory and Kevin? I wanted to ask but didn't.

Slowly, Ryan raised his hand up from where it rested in his lap and placed it on my forearm. He didn't squeeze or pat, he just let it rest there for a moment. It felt warm, even through the wool of my coat.

"I'm really glad you're my friend," he said, finally breaking the silence. "I like when you drive me home."

"Me too," I replied.

He pulled his hand back and opened the door. Stepping out, he closed it behind him. I watched him walk up the yard to his house, giving me a small wave before stepping inside the door like he always did. I pulled away from the curb and headed down the street home. As I drove, I could still feel his hand pressed against my forearm.

15

When I got home, my parents were fighting. Or it seemed like they were. I came in the front door and I could hear them when I walked in, their voices coming heavy and deep from the kitchen. There was no yelling. As I passed through the doorway that led from the foyer to the living room, I could hear their voices a little clearer. They apparently didn't know I was home. I glanced into the kitchen and could see their bodies reflected in the window above the sink. It looked like they were standing next to the kitchen table. My mom was looking at my father who was looking away at the wall.

"What do you want, Saul?" her voice was calm and steady.

"I don't know." For once, my father didn't sound angry. He sounded tired. I could almost hear the sound of him closing his eyes.

My mom sighed, "Just tell me what you want and I'll do it. I'm ready now."

I paused, my stomach dropping. She was ready?

Turning, I quietly crept up the stairs. All the lights were off. I felt along the dark hallway to the door to my room, stepping inside and shutting the door. Silence echoed within the four walls. I left the light off and laid down on my bed. Shadows from the tree outside the window crept across the ceiling. The air felt cold and dry.

This was different. Their voices sounded different. Was this it? Was this when it all finally happened? I thought about all the time I'd spent hoping, praying that this would happen. All the nights I'd spent in my room listening to their voices coming up from downstairs, feeling the air thickening with them. So much time had been spent praying for some kind of break and now? Now it felt different than I had thought it would. I thought I would feel relief, but there was a different feeling in my stomach. It was one I didn't like. For the first time, I felt scared.

Until then, I had never thought about what would happen when all that tension that had been building up finally went away. I had imagined that things would feel lighter, like our house would open up and the air would be clearer. My mom would be happier, and she would smile more and laugh more. But I had never thought about what it all really meant. My parents would be separating, divorcing eventually. My father would move out and he would find a new place to live. Would I see him again or would he just disappear from our lives? Would he ask me to come stay with him? I couldn't imagine going and living with my father. Even though I loved him, I just couldn't imagine leaving my mom so I could live with him. There wasn't a life with him. My father and I didn't relate to each other in any way. When it came down to it, I had a life with my mom. We talked and played board games and went to see movies together. I didn't have that with my father. He worked and we had the occasional conversation in the kitchen, but there wasn't much more than that. We didn't talk the way Mom and I did. Plus, how could he expect me to live with him after how he'd treated Mom? After the things he'd said to her? I couldn't live with that. It would be like a betrayal. I would be betraying my mom.

I sighed deeply and looked around my room. Getting up, I stepped around my bed, opening the closet door and sitting down. I breathed deeply, trying to clear my head. Everything felt heavy and I needed to find a way to get out of my mind. Brooke helped with that. I picked up my flashlight and turned it on, shining it at the wall. Had Brooke gone through something like this? Were her parents still together? Was that why they'd moved? I looked over her words, reading each one slowly. Eventually I landed on one.

The sound of the front door closing rose to my ears. I leaned out of my closet and listened. Silence. Standing up and moving towards the door to my room, I opened it and stepped out. As I moved down the stairs, I felt the thickness in the air. It wasn't as thick as it had been after their normal fights. It was stuffy, but somehow clear. I saw the light coming from the kitchen as I reached the bottom step. In the reflection of the window, I could see my mom sitting at the table now. I couldn't see my father. I stepped into the room.

The room was dark around the edges, all the light coming from the lamp that hung down from the ceiling above the table. It was harsh and bright, covering the table and chairs completely. The lamp hung still, like the light over a suspect being interrogated. Each flaw and imperfection in the wood of the table stood out, vulnerable and exposed. The flowers that stood in their glass vase at the center of the table were finally starting to wilt. Our orange placemats sat neatly along each side. Loosely crumpled tissues were strewn across the placemat at the end of the table closest to the outside door. That was where my mom was sitting when I entered the room. She was sitting sideways on the chair as I approached her, facing me. Her eyes were red, her lips in a flat line. I stopped next to the table.

"What's wrong?" I knew what was wrong, but I couldn't find any other words.

"Everything." She stared off into space, her eyes lost in the salt and pepper shakers on the counter across the room by the stove. Dishes from the spaghetti she'd made for dinner were piled in the sink. I could see spaghetti sauce in a puddle on the top plate, shining slightly in the glow of the light.

I turned back to her, "What happened?"

She put both hands on the table, gently rubbing them across the placemat, flattening the wrinkles and creases. "You know, I think I've known it was coming for quite a while now. It was inevitable, really. I tried to deny it, ignore it, put it off for as long as possible, but it was always going to happen."

She was silent for a few moments, breathing deeply and closing her eyes. There was clarity in her breathing. I knew she was hurting, but there was a kind of relief in the muscles of her face.

"Did he leave?" I asked quietly.

"Yes." Just like that, I could take a breath.

"Is he coming back?"

"Yes, but only for a little while." Another breath.

"What made this happen? What were you fighting about?"

She opened her eyes again, "The same thing we've always been fighting about. Each other."

I gripped the back of the chair next to me. This was it. This was the moment everything would change. "Is this real?"

Lifting her hand, she rubbed at her forehead. "Yes, it's real."

She stared down at the tabletop, eyes moving over the wood. Stepping forward, I stood next to her. What would happen now? What was the next step? I stayed silent, not wanting to overwhelm her with my questions and uncertainty. She reached up and took my hand, holding it tightly in hers. She was going to need me now. Everything would start changing and I would be there for her. I could take care of her, help her through this.

Things had finally become too much, piled too high. I thought back to my closet upstairs, to what Brooke had left on the wall.

The dam finally broke.

16

It felt weird going back to school at the end of winter break. Nobody knew about my parents, but I did. I could feel them on my shoulders as I got out of the car and walked into the building. The weight of their separation was more than I had expected it to be. I had always imagined this would be a good thing, that I would feel happy. Instead I just felt tired and lonely and so separate from everyone else around me. It was weird, walking through the halls with everyone when I felt like I had this big secret on my back, which was strange since it wasn't a secret. I could tell someone. I had already told Kevin, Mallory, and Ryan. The morning after it all happened, I had sent them a text to tell them. They had immediately driven over to my house and picked me up and taken me to get lunch. We sat in Mallory's car and ate, and I told them everything that happened.

"Do you think there's any chance they'll get back together? Maybe it's just a trial separation." Mallory had said, but I assured her it wasn't.

"It's been coming for a while. I knew it would come at some point, but it still feels so strange now that it's actually happening." I had been trying to get rid of the twisting in my stomach since the night before.

"I mean, just because you knew it was coming doesn't mean it's not still gonna hit you," Kevin added. "You can prepare yourself for it, but that doesn't mean you won't get hurt."

"I know," I said, leaning back in the seat. Ryan was sitting next to me and I could see him look at me out of the corner of my eye.

"I'm sorry that you're hurting." I turned to him and he looked back at me with those big blue eyes. We sat there staring at each other for a minute and for the briefest moment I felt it all disappear. All I could see were his eyes, all I could feel was them gazing into mine. And then, as quick as it had left, it all came back. I took a deep breath and sat up straight again.

"Thank you," I said, lingering in his eyes before turning back to the bag of fries in my lap. We finished our lunch before going to the Empty Cup for a while. Later in the afternoon they took me home.

My father was sitting on the couch when I walked in the living room. He looked up at me, "Hey."

"Hey."

His eyes stayed on me as I made my way across the room to the kitchen. I poured myself a glass of water and walked back through the living room to the stairs. I could feel his eyes on me as I walked. What was he expecting me to do or say? I didn't want to say anything, didn't even really want to talk to him.

"Hey, son," I turned as he spoke. He leaned forward onto his knees, placing the remote on the coffee table in front of him. "I, uh, I just . . . I just want to make sure you're okay with everything that's going on between me and your mother. None of it's your fault, I promise." He looked up at me as if I were supposed to have a response to this, to him. This was the most father-like thing he'd said to me in a while. Did he think that this sudden urge to parent was going to get a reaction from me?

"I know. I'm fine." I said, before turning away from him and walking up the stairs to my room. I shut the door, grabbed my notebook, and sat down in the bottom of my closet. My hand moved quickly across the page as I began working on a scene where Connor has a big fight with his brother. Gripping the pencil tightly, I filled up seven whole pages before I realized my pencil was starting to crack. Setting it down with my notebook, I twisted my wrist around to flex the muscles. I felt hot and annoyed. This wasn't what I had expected. I should have been feeling happy, not pissed off. My father didn't understand. He thought he could just say stuff like that, pretend to be engaged with my life, and that it made up for everything? After all the shit he put my mother through, it wasn't going to be that simple. He didn't get to just leave us and think things were going to be fine. It wasn't fine.

I looked over the wall at Brooke's words, trying to find something that I could connect with, something that would help me make sense of everything.

These were supposed to be the best years of my life

That's what they told us, isn't it, Brooke? That's the lie. Although, frankly, compared to everything I was seeing happen with all the adults in my life, maybe these *were* the best years. Maybe everything just got harder after this. I didn't want to think about that being true. Everything seemed so hard right now, what would I do when it all got worse? I looked at people like my mom and Jeremy and wondered how they were able to deal with the problems that kept coming into their lives. It just seemed like this never-ending rain cloud was hovering over them.

My head hurt so I went to bed early. When I woke up in the morning, I felt less frustrated, but the headache remained. I wanted to be past that, to get to the part where it was good, and my mom was happy, and everything seemed right. As I pulled into the school parking lot an hour later, I felt like that would be a long time away.

Taking my books from my locker, I made my way to Mrs. Stroud's class. She was sitting at her desk rummaging through a stack of papers. The sleeves of her oversized red sweater were pushed back up her arms. She looked up as I walked in and sat down at a desk.

"Good morning, how was your break?" Reaching across her desk, she picked up her blue thermos and took a sip.

"It was okay." Now, more than ever, I wanted to keep her separate from everything else. "How was yours?"

"Oh, it was really nice actually. After Christmas, we went to Niagara Falls for a couple days. Alexander has been wanting to go for years, but we just never had a chance. It was so beautiful there. I'll have to bring in the pictures when we get them printed." She stopped talking for a second and looked at me, "Are you all right?"

I must have had a strange expression on my face without realizing it because she was looking at me as though I was about to throw up. "Yeah, I'm fine. I'm just really tired."

"Are you sure? You can talk to me if you need to, you know that, right?" She stood up and walked around to the front of her desk.

"Yeah, I'm okay. I promise." I lied.

"All right. Do you have any new pages for me?"

I reached into my folder and pulled the eighteen pages I had typed up the previous night. She took them and flipped through them before placing them on her desk.

"Good work. I'll look at them this week." She stepped back around her desk and picked up a piece of chalk, writing out the homework for that evening in the corner of the board.

I reached into my bag, pulling out my textbook and notepad. As the rest of the class began to come in, I closed my eyes and took a deep breath.

17

For the past couple weeks, my mom had been acting like nothing happened. Every day, she'd gotten up and gone to work and come home like it was just a normal day. When she made dinner, she still made enough for my father. We didn't eat together anymore though. Mom and I would eat as soon as dinner was ready, even if my father was going to be home soon. Most nights, he stayed at work even later than normal.

My father had begun looking for another place to live. On his days off he went out to meet a realtor. He never talked about places he saw or whether he'd found one. He would just come home and lay on the couch, going from watching TV to napping.

Neither of them talked much. Occasionally my mom would ask me about school or my friends, but other than that there was mostly silence. It was a strange contrast to go from the fighting every other day to complete and total silence. It wasn't the kind of change I'd expected. The quiet was almost uncomfortable. I didn't know what to say to either of them or whether I should even speak at all. They both seemed to prefer the quiet and I didn't want to ruin that. And yet, it almost started to drive me a little crazy. It felt almost as suffocating as the sound of them fighting and I hated it. Was this what things were going to be like from now on? Were we just going to go from one extreme to the other? I wasn't sure I could handle that.

On Thursday, I went with Mallory, Theo, and Ryan to the bowling alley. Kevin was working a closing shift. We played a couple games together and I was actually able to have fun. I hadn't been bowling since I was a kid and found that I was surprisingly good at it.

Theo was the best though. He got six strikes in the two hours we were playing. Every time it happened, he would just turn and shrug like he didn't mean to do it. Mallory would just start laughing.

"You're some kind of freak, you know that?" she said as we ordered another round of fries from the concession stand. Her dark hair was hanging around her face and she lifted a hand to push it back, rolling her eyes. "Nobody should be that good at bowling."

"I just let go of the ball," Theo replied, twisting his mouth as he gave her another shrug. "I don't choose where it goes."

"Oh, whatever!" she exclaimed, slapping one of his broad shoulders with the back of her hand.

Theo grabbed it and held it above her head, bringing his fingers up to tickle her armpit. Mallory jerked away from him, squealing.

Ryan and I walked back over to our lane, sitting down in the uncomfortable wooden chairs that were chipping green paint onto the floor. The lights shining down from the ceiling were various shades of blue and pink and purple.

"How are things with your parents?" Ryan asked, turning to look at me with his bright blue eyes. He was wearing a maroon zip-up hoodie that was slightly too big and hung loosely around his shoulders.

I sighed, "They're okay, I guess. It's been pretty quiet lately, mostly because they're not talking to each other."

"Is that better than how it was?"

"I don't really know yet."

I looked around at all the people eating and bowling, laughing and smiling. There was a little boy, probably no older than six or seven, walking up to the line to make his move. I watched as he held the ball with two hands, lowering it back between his legs before tossing it out in front of him. It made a loud thump as it hit the lane, rolling forward quickly before slowing down. The little boy stood there as the ball got closer and closer to hitting the pins. Finally it reached the end of the lane, knocking down two pins before rolling off to the side and into the gutter. The little boy threw his arms up into the air and turned back to smile at his mom and dad, who ran up and gave him a big hug.

"Can I ask you something?" I said, turning back to look at Ryan who was staring at the little boy as well.

"Sure."

"Why don't we ever go to your house? We've been to mine and Kevin's, and I've seen Mallory's, but we never go to yours."

His eyes stayed on the little boy for a few moments and I could see his body inhale and exhale. He finally dropped his gaze down to his lap.

"When I'm at home, my parents are always watching me. I can feel them waiting to see if I'll do it again." One hand came up to wipe at some invisible spot on his knee. "I know what I did hurt them, but it's just tiring sometimes."

I thought about my own home and how many times over the past few months I'd chosen to go out with my friends so I could get away from what was going on with my parents. Ryan didn't want them watching him, but I didn't want to watch my parents.

"Do you ever feel like you want to do it again?"

He shook his head, "No."

"Good. I like having you around."

Ryan looked up and away, but he had a smile on his face.

I meant what I said. Even though he didn't talk much, there was something nice about always having him there. I didn't know why, but I felt comfortable around him, even more so than with Kevin or Mallory.

When Theo and Mallory came back over, we started a new game. I was first so I stood and picked up the green ball from the rack. Stepping toward the line, I looked back. Mallory and Theo were talking and eating fries. Ryan was watching me. I turned back to the lane and swung the ball. I hit five pins.

18

That Saturday, I went over to Mallory's house to pick her up. We were going over to Kevin's and her car was in the shop, so I offered to pick her and Ryan up.

She lived in a two-story brick house that looked similar to mine. Her parents were both at work. They were dentists.

The inside of the house was pretty nice, very beige, very minimal clutter. There were pictures of her and her parents up on the wall. She looked like both of them, same dark hair and blue eyes. All the pictures showed them smiling at the beach, at a family picnic, on a ski slope. It was a picture-perfect family.

I followed her up to her bedroom so she could get her shoes. The last time I'd been here we'd only hung out in the living room, so I was excited to see her space.

The walls of her room were red, black picture frames spread out every few feet showing images of mountains or a child laughing. Most of them were in black and white.

"These are beautiful." I said, stepping over to one of an old woman, assumedly a grandparent, who was gazing out a window.

Mallory sat down on the bed, which was covered in a white duvet. There were books on her nightstand.

"Thanks," she said, leaning down to lace up her sneakers. "They're from a couple years ago. I should really change them out."

"They're so good." I turned to one showing the same window the woman was looking out of. She was gone and the window was open, the curtain frozen in the air. "You're so talented. I can't believe you're not going to keep up with this next year."

I heard her sigh and turned to look at her. She was standing up next to the bed now, hands on her hips, looking at the picture.

"I'm sorry, I don't want to make you mad. It's just that you're so good at this and you're just pushing it to the side."

She rolled her eyes at me, "I'm not pushing it to the side. It's just not going to be my main focus. I have to make a living somehow and photography can't do that."

"When you're this good, I'm sure you can find a job."

Walking over to her desk, a small wooden table in the corner, she picked up her bag. "Come on, let's go."

"Wait," I reached out for her arm. She stopped and turned around.

"I don't want to talk about this, okay?" She looked me in the eye, lifting a hand to run her fingers through her hair. "I'm so tired of talking about this. I just want you guys to accept my decision."

"I just want to *understand* your decision. Some of the stuff you do just doesn't make sense to me."

"Like what?" she asked, crossing her arms over her chest and leaning back against the door frame.

"Like," I thought about how to say what I wanted to say. "Like, why are you doing this thing with Theo? He's leaving in two months. Why are you getting with him when you know he's going away?"

"I can't live my life waiting for Kevin." she replied, cutting me off.

"That's not what I'm saying. You don't have to wait for Kevin. I just don't know why you're getting into a relationship with someone that's not going to be here in a few months. You may never see him again." I could see her jaw tightening. She didn't want to talk about this, but I needed her to. I needed her to tell me why she was going through with this thing that seemed completely pointless to me.

"So? I'm not getting attached. I told you that." She moved past me to the bed and sat down.

I sat down next to her, "Yes, you are. I don't think you care about him the way you care about Kevin, but you're definitely attached. I can see it when you guys are together. You act like he's really your boyfriend."

I looked at her. She was staring at the floor, arms still crossed at her chest. She didn't respond.

"Mallory?"

"I don't need him." Her voice was quiet now, anger gone.

"Theo?"

"Kevin."

"What do you mean?" I turned my body so I was facing her.

Her jaw clenched. "I don't need Kevin. That's why I'm with Theo."

"I don't understand."

She closed her eyes and took a deep breath, "I needed to prove that I didn't need him."

"Prove it to who?"

"To myself." Mallory pushed a strand of hair behind her ear. "When I was growing up, my mom taught me that I shouldn't need anyone. She said everyone should be dependent on themselves and no one else." In her lap she ran the fingers of one hand over the knuckles of the other, over and over the lumps. "Last year, I realized that my want for him was starting to feel like need."

"So you got with Theo because . . .?"

"Because if I could date Theo, it might mean that I didn't need Kevin."

I realized then that the anger Mallory was showing wasn't for me. It was for herself.

"I'm not over Kevin and I hate it. This isn't how I'm supposed to be. It's pathetic."

"No, it's not." I lifted my arm to her back and left it there. "It's not pathetic."

"Yes, it is. It's pathetic. And it's worse that I brought Theo into this."

"But you do care about him."

"I know. I really, *really* like him. But not the way I like Kevin."

"He doesn't have to know that. You said he didn't want something serious, and you do like him, so just enjoy being together."

She looked at me, worry in her blue eyes. "Does this make me a bad person? Dating someone I know I can't love?"

I raised my arm from her back to her shoulder and pulled her into me, leaning my head against hers. She nestled into my shoulder.

"No, it doesn't make you a bad person."

At Kevin's we all sat around and watched a movie. He had to go to work for the evening shift, so we couldn't do much else. After the movie was over, I went to use the bathroom.

The bathroom was small like the rest of the apartment, with only a toilet and sink contained within the baby blue walls. There were small scratches and marks on the paint. One spot at the bottom near the baseboard was a faded orange, almost like Kool-Aid. The carpeted floors brushed beneath my shoes with every step. There was a smell of air disinfectant lingering in the small space. Small, yellow hand towels hung from a rack on the wall.

Buckling my belt, I turned to wash my hands in the short, porcelain sink. Cool water ran between my fingers as I rubbed them together. Reaching up, I squirted a bit of hand soap and lathered it between my palms. There was a gold framed photo of a couple, that I assumed to be Kevin's parents, sitting next to the faucet. They were sitting at a table at what seemed to be a wedding reception, maybe *their* wedding reception. Each had a glass of champagne in their hand and was smiling at the other.

I couldn't begin to imagine what it felt like to lose your parents. The thought was inconceivable to me. Kevin somehow managed to find a way to be okay again, but I didn't know how he did it. Sure, he had Jeremy with him, but that wasn't the same. Jeremy would never be able to take the role that a parent is supposed to have in your life. I thought about my own parents in their broken state. Even if they weren't together anymore, they were still there. I could still see them and talk to them. As much resentment as I had for my father, he was still there if I needed him. I could still go to him if I needed help. Kevin didn't have that, and he never would again.

"Are you done yet?"

I was pulled out of my thoughts by a voice on the other side of the wall. It was Jeremy, only his friendly tone was gone, exasperation taking its place.

I quickly placed the towel that I'd been using to dry my hands back on the rack, "Oh, uh, yeah, I— "

"Yes, I know that."

He wasn't speaking to me.

Opening the bathroom door, I stepped out into the hall. To the right of the bathroom was another door that was slightly ajar. Stepping towards it, I peered through the crack.

It was an office. Two bookshelves stood on either side of an open window, harsh sunlight pouring into the room. In front of the window was a large, wooden desk that faced the rest of the room. Open envelopes and ripped up papers were spread across the desktop. A small computer monitor sat on the far corner, screen-light shining down on the keyboard. There was a round, glass paperweight resting atop a black, leather-bound book. The sun from the window illuminated the gold glitter that hovered inside the ball.

Jeremy sat behind the desk in a black chair. There was a phone to his ear as he leaned back, his other hand gripping the black hair on the top of his head. His brow was furrowed, the creases and worry lines in his face even more pronounced. He stared down at the edge of his desk as he listened to whatever the person on the other end of the line was saying.

"I know that. I know that" he gestured with his hand out in front of him as if he were talking to someone on the other side of the desk. "But I don't have any other options . . . We're trying for scholarships, but there's no guarantee."

Kevin. College.

"Well, we wouldn't be having this conversation if you people hadn't taken our house away!" He brought his hand to the bridge of his nose and squeezed, "Yes, I know that. I didn't mean . . . it's just that we wouldn't be having this problem if the foreclosure hadn't happened. I know there was nothing you could do, but there was nothing I could do either. I'm trying to get things in a good place with our finances, but it's hard with that hanging over our heads . . . Yes, we're in an apartment now."

He stood, pacing back and forth next to his desk. His free hand went from his hip to his forehead to knead the skin there.

"But . . . please, there has to be some way for us to make this happen . . . You don't understand. I *need* this for him. I *need* to give him this." He had stopped pacing and was staring down at the envelopes and letters on his desk, "He's such a good kid. I mean he really is. He works his ass off trying to help me out with the bills and never complains. Not once, never. Every other kid his age is out partying and hanging with friends, but, most nights, he's working or cooking dinner so *I* can work. He hasn't gotten to have the kind of life that you and I probably had as teenagers. He hasn't gotten the chance to just be stupid for a night. This could be his chance. College could be his chance to have that." His eyes were closed now as he stood there. "He wants to major in engineering. This is something he's been working towards for so long and I can't tell him now that it's not an option. Please . . ."

Silence as he listened to the voice on the other end. His head fell to his chest.

"Yeah, okay . . . no, I know."

Bad news.

"Okay, thank you anyway." He pressed the button to end the call and dropped the phone onto the desk. He stood there motionless for several seconds. When the anger came into his face, I saw it. His lips drew a tight line across his face, jaw setting firm. He balled his hands into fists and released them several times as his breathing became shorter and faster. When he finally burst, he gripped the side corners of his desk and kicked it repeatedly. The bang of shoe against wood echoed in the room as he kept kicking and kicking and kicking. I looked back down the hall to see if Kevin had heard, but the TV was too loud. He finally stopped when a small piece of wood broke off of one corner. Falling to his knees, he continued to hold his tight grip on the desk corner. His teeth were clenched tight as his lips were pulled back. His eyes burned a hole in the side of the desk, the corners glistening slightly.

Slowly, his back slowed down as his breathing came back down to normal. He unclenched his teeth, opening his mouth to lick his lips before pulling them back into a firm line. His gaze was still on the desk when I stepped away.

As I made my way back to the living room, I thought about Kevin. Jeremy was right, he worked so hard to help them. He had spent so much time working so they could have money to pay the bills, to get their finances to a place that would allow him to go away. We'd spent so much time talking about college and now that might not even be a possibility for him?

And Jeremy. He'd taken over the role of parent in Kevin's life. What life would he be living if he hadn't had to take care of things for Kevin? Would he be married? Have a kid of his own? Jeremy talked about all the experiences that Kevin wasn't getting to have as a teenager, but wasn't it the same for himself? He had given up his life to come back home. I was sure he didn't resent Kevin for that, but I wondered if he ever thought about where he would be if it had never happened. How could he not?

It just didn't seem fair for all this shit to keep happening to them. Wasn't losing your parents enough? Why did they have to struggle for so long afterwards, scared that they would get their home taken away again, scared that they would be stuck like this forever?

When I got to the couch, I sat down between Mallory and Ryan. Kevin leaned forward from Mallory's other side.

"Did you fall in?"

I looked at him, hoping that he couldn't tell that I had just seen something that wasn't meant for me to see.

"Yeah," I replied, faking a laugh. "It was horrible."

19

When my father moved out a couple weeks later, it was surprisingly peaceful. He didn't take a lot of things with him, just clothes and a couple pictures. I half expected him to sit me down for some kind of talk, but he didn't even do that. Maybe he knew I didn't want to talk. Maybe he didn't know what to say.

It was a Sunday afternoon and all the lights were off. The sun shone through my bedroom window turning my walls orange. I was sitting on my bed writing, the sounds of my father packing coming through the open door. I listened as he shoved clothes into his duffel bag and put picture frames into a box.

My mom was working. She'd requested a shift since she knew he'd be packing up. I'd stayed, for reasons I didn't really know. I was meeting up with my friends later in the afternoon, but I could have gone anywhere. Instead, I stayed and listened to him pack.

It didn't make me feel sad or angry like I thought it might. All the movies showed the kid getting upset or furious, but I didn't feel that. I didn't really feel anything. It was just happening.

After he'd taken the last box to the car, he came back upstairs and stopped in my doorway.

"I'm leaving now. I think I've got everything I need." He watched his shoes as he spoke, and I wondered what he was feeling.

"Okay." I didn't know what else to say.

"Listen, once I get my apartment set up, I thought maybe you could come over for dinner. Or we can go out. Whatever you want." His eyes went from his shoes to the window, squinting in the sunlight. I watched as he lifted one hand and ran it through his black hair. He still didn't look at me.

"Okay, I guess." The thought of having dinner with my father wasn't very exciting, but I couldn't really say no.

"All right, well, I love you, son." He finally looked at me and his mouth turned down slightly in a frown. It looked like he wanted to say something else, the way his mouth hung open slightly. Instead, he stayed silent.

"Love you too."

He nodded slowly and turned back into the hallway. I listened to his footsteps go down the stairs, getting quieter as they moved through the house and to the door. There was a soft thud as it closed behind him.

I sat there, my pencil in hand, and listened to the silence of the house. The air felt different. It felt like something was missing, something that had always been there, and I didn't know whether I missed it or not.

That night, we all went to see a movie. Mallory had gotten a gift card from some relative for Christmas and decided to treat everyone. The movie was pretty good, and everyone seemed to have fun.

As we all made our way out into the parking lot at the end of the night, I watched Mallory take off running with Theo following close behind. Ryan and Kevin stood at my sides as we watched Theo catch up to her and pick her up, tossing her over his shoulder before turning to run back toward us. Mallory laughed loudly as she bounced on Theo's shoulder with every step he took.

I turned to look at Kevin and found him watching them. He had found out about the financial aid problems that Jeremy had been talking about on the phone. For the most part, he seemed to be taking it okay. He'd told us that he was going to study harder so he could keep up his grades enough to hopefully apply for some extra scholarships. It was nice to see him acting so optimistic about something so serious, but I could tell it was still weighing on him. His body seemed more tense lately, his usual friendly manner dampened slightly.

"She's happy." he said, "She really is."

I wanted to tell him what she'd told me, tell him that she wasn't as happy as she looked, that she was trying to find happiness in anything she could. Instead, I just looked back at Theo running through the parking lot with Mallory slung over his shoulder, her laugh echoing out through the air.

That night I woke up around 1 a.m. to go to the bathroom. On my way back, I stopped by my mom's closed bedroom door. I thought I would hear her soft snoring, but instead I heard her crying.

I met my father at an Olive Garden for dinner on a Saturday. I spent the whole afternoon dreading it. We weren't meeting until six o'clock, so I had to spend an entire afternoon just sitting around waiting. Homework was only able to distract me until I finished it and then had to find something else to take its place. Writing just wouldn't happen. I spent most of the afternoon after my homework was finished just laying on my bed. My mom was at work until eight, so I was alone.

I hadn't seen him in a month. He hadn't come by since the day he moved out. There were still a few of his things there, mostly just pictures and a few knick-knacks that I kept expecting him to come pick up at some point, but never did. Other than the occasional text message asking how I was doing, I hadn't seen or heard from him.

Part of me was curious. Would he look different? Would he act different? Did getting out of the house and leaving us change who he was as a person? It occurred to me that he could be an entirely different person now. He could be more outgoing, talk more, laugh more. Maybe he picked up new hobbies. Or just hobbies. He never had hobbies to begin with. Maybe he was crafty now. He had always been good at helping me with school projects. What if he had a whole new personality? Could he have changed that much in a month?

As I spent the afternoon sprawled out across my bed, I wondered whether it was true. Could one month away from us change him? I wasn't any different. At least not in a way that I could tell.

And even if he was different, would it matter? I tried to imagine a world where he left and became someone new, someone I could talk to and relate to. I tried to imagine having that father-son relationship that we had somehow missed out on, but I couldn't. I couldn't picture us sitting down over a bowl of pasta and talking about things that fathers and sons talked about. What *did* they talk about? Sports? Girls? I couldn't really bring anything to the table on either topic so it wouldn't matter anyway. Because isn't that it? Isn't that how it's supposed to be? Aren't we supposed to toss a football around in the front yard and talk about how to ask out a girl? That's what they showed me on TV.

At a quarter to six, I reluctantly got up and left. As I got in the car, I received a text from my mom:

Mom: *It'll be fine. I love you.*

The Olive Garden we were meeting at was only a few blocks away, so it didn't take me long to get there. I sat in my car in the silence and waited for him to show up. There was a couple that stepped out of the restaurant with their little girl swinging between them, one hand in each of theirs. They looked down at her as they crossed the parking lot, smiles on their faces. It was clear they adored her. She looked up at them as they swung her into the air and giggled which brought out a laugh in each of them. As they reached their car which was across from mine and began buckling her into her car seat, the husband placed a hand on his wife's back and rubbed gently. Before the wife went around to get in the passenger seat, he kissed her lightly on the nose and smiled. They were a perfect little family. What were we?

A few yards away, I saw my father pull into a parking space. The car turned off and he got out. As he stood and walked around to the front of his car, looking around for mine, I realized he didn't look any different. He still wore the same clothes. He still combed his hair the same way. He still had the five o'clock shadow. Physically, he was exactly the same person that had walked out the door a month earlier.

His eyes eventually landed on my car and the corners of his mouth turned up just slightly. He waved as I turned off my ignition and got out. Did I look different to him?

"Hey," he said, walking over to me. There. It was something different in his walk. His shoulders, maybe. There was something . . . *easier* about the way he moved, something lighter.

"Hi." I replied as he leaned in for a hug. His hugs were the same.

We turned to walk inside, "How are you?"

"I'm okay," I answered, holding the door open for him. "How are you?"

"Oh, you know, just still trying to get everything set up at my new place. You should come over sometime and see it. I think you'd like it."

"Yeah, sure. Sounds good."

The hostess led us to a booth toward the back. A bright light hung down from the ceiling, giving the small space an investigative feel. I took a menu from the hostess and looked at it for several minutes, not focusing on anything except a reason to not speak for a few moments. He did the same. The waitress came over and took our drink order, two waters, and went away.

I looked up at my father over the menu. His eyes were focused on the paper but didn't move. They just hovered in the middle somewhere. His eyebrows were furrowed like he was thinking about something.

The waitress brought our water as well as a basket of breadsticks. As soon as she walked away, I snatched one up and started eating it, trying to find something else that would give me a reason to not say anything. My father looked up at me and laughed a bit.

"Hungry?" He asked, picking a breadstick up and placing it on a napkin. Pulling off a chunk, he tossed it in his mouth.

"Yeah," I laughed. "Sorry."

We sat there for a few minutes, just eating quietly. He kept his eyes down on his breadstick, almost comfortable in the silence. I realized that nothing was different at all. We were still exactly the same. This was exactly like every dinner we had together for the past several years. Just eating quietly.

Part of me had wanted it to be different. There was a part of me that really wanted something to have changed. I didn't want to admit it, but I had hoped that he somehow figured out how to be a dad during the past month. But maybe that wasn't possible. Maybe we would never be what we were supposed to be. I wondered if it was pointless to even hope that he would be able to change.

I looked at him as he sat there eating. He didn't look at me or say anything. Should I? Should I be the one to initiate things? How? I didn't know where to begin or what to say first. Part of me was frustrated that I was the one who would have to push things, that I would have to make the first move if I wanted any kind of relationship with him. Why couldn't he do it? He was the father so shouldn't he be the one to make the first effort? Why did it have to be me? I didn't know what to do or where to start. Every question or sentence that came into my head seemed stupid or weird.

"So, how's work?" I asked finally, making a move.

"Oh, it's fine." He glanced up at me before looking back down at his hands as they pulled off another bit of breadstick. "Long hours. Not much has changed since I, uh . . . since I moved."

The waitress came to take our order.

"You know, Peter," my father began after the waitress walked away. "I'd really like for us to have dinner again."

"Okay." I replied. This time was going so well he wanted to do it again?

"I mean, I want to make this a regular thing."

I looked at him again and his eyes were on mine. He still seemed just as uncomfortable as I was, but I could tell he was serious about what he said and wanted me to know that. Was this his move?

"Yeah, okay."

Part of me was curious about what would happen if we started having dinner together more often, whether that would help our relationship at all. It seemed like a long shot considering how awkward things were, but it seemed right to give it a shot.

After dinner, I went home to check on mom before going back out to meet my friends. I found her in her bedroom, sorting mail at her desk. Her back was to the door, red hair going dark as the light from her desk lamp made a silhouette of her body.

"Hey."

She turned back and looked at me quickly before shoving her finger into the fold of an envelope, ripping it open.

"Hi."

"You okay?"

"Yeah, I'm just trying to see if any of this mail is important."

Her voice was rough and thick, and I could tell she'd been crying before I came home. That had been happening more and more lately, the crying. It wasn't something she did in front of me, but I could always tell when she had been. She would come downstairs in the morning for breakfast and her eyes would be red. Make up covered some of it, but I could still tell. Most often, she cried at night. I could hear her sniffling through the walls.

I thought my father leaving would make her feel better. She wouldn't have to deal with him coming home late or worry about getting into another fight. She could finally have the peace I craved as well. But that wasn't the case. She seemed almost more upset now that he was gone than when she had to deal with the fights.

"What did you have for dinner?" I asked, hoping casual conversation would help clear her head.

"I didn't eat anything. I don't really have an appetite right now." she replied.

"You should eat something. Do you want me to heat up the leftover pasta?"

She leaned forward and I could see her hand come up to wipe at her face. "No, I'll just eat a salad later. I've had too many carbs lately. How was dinner with your dad?"

She turned around in her chair to look at me and I could see her red face.

"It was fine. We ate and then left. Didn't last too long."

"Do you think he'll ask you to do it again?" Her voice was soft despite the roughness coming from her throat.

"Yeah, he already asked if we could keep doing it. I think he wants to make it a regular thing." I kept my voice casual, like it didn't really matter. I didn't want her to know how curious I was about what things would be like between my father and me if we started having regular dinners together. She didn't need to worry about me right now.

"Oh, well that's good."

"Yeah. I'm gonna go meet up with my friends. Let me know if you need anything." I gave her a friendly smile before turning and walking back down the hallway. I could hear her sigh as I began walking down the stairs.

I drove to the mall to meet Kevin, Mallory, and Ryan at the food court. Kevin was working a closing shift and had a half hour for dinner. They were all crowded around a table near the McDonald's. Textbooks were spread out across it, taking up almost every inch except for where paper drink cups were sitting. Kevin was bent over one, highlighting an entire paragraph of text. Mallory and Ryan sat across from him. They each had a stack of index cards in front of them.

"Hey." I said, pulling up the chair next to Kevin and plopping down in it with a sigh.

Mallory looked up at me from across the table, "Hey! What's up?"

"Dinner with father dearest." I replied.

"Oh, gosh, I totally forgot that was tonight. How'd it go?"

"Exactly how I thought it would." I said, leaning my head back and closing my eyes.

She sighed, "I'm really sorry, Peter."

"It's fine. It doesn't matter anyway." I sat up in the chair and looked at all the textbooks spread out on the table. "What's all this?"

"We're helping Kevin study. I found out about this scholarship that's available through the Arlington Foundation that's focused on helping students who are really smart and hardworking but are in a lower income situation. They hold an exam every April and the five students who score the highest get a full-ride scholarship to apply to whatever school they choose." She smiled. "It's perfect for Kevin."

"Only if I can pass the damn thing," Kevin added, making a note in his notebook. His black uniform hat was turned backwards, pressing down against his curly hair.

"You'll pass!" Mallory replied, tossing a balled-up piece of paper at him, and hitting him right on the nose.

He looked up at her, "Do you realize how many other people are going to be taking this test? Last year they had three hundred qualifying candidates. I have to be one of the top five out of *all* of them."

"And you *won't* be with *that* attitude. We're going to help you, Kevin. We're going to make sure you're prepared to do the best job you can. Just have faith in yourself. *I* do." Mallory stared at him across the table.

We all did. Nothing in Kevin's life had gone as planned. From his parent's death, to the money troubles he and Jeremy were always having to deal with, to this. Nothing seemed to go his way. Most of the time, he seemed to accept it and smile anyway. But, every now and then, you could see it weighing on him. Sometimes it finally got through his positivity and sat there on his shoulder, bringing him down.

"We're making flashcards," Ryan said, looking up with bright eyes.

I smiled at him and pulled one of Kevin's notebooks over to me. "So, what parts do you need to know?"

He looked at the notebook in my hand, "All of it."

Reaching over, I grabbed a stack of index cards and a pen, "Well, I guess I should get started."

We sat there for a while in silence. Kevin made notes from his textbooks while the rest of us made flashcards for him. Looking through his notes, I felt a weight on my heart. There was a lot of information there that he was going to have to learn and memorize in time for the test. I tried to suppress the worry that he wouldn't be able to do it. He needed to do it, he had to. It was the only option left now for him to get the rest of the money he needed to go to Stanford, his top choice out of the schools he'd applied to.

My phone rang and I pulled it out of my pocket. It was Mom.

"Hey, Mom." I answered.

"Hey, Peter, where are you?" My mother's voice came through the speaker shaky and full of tears. Had something happened with my father?

"I'm at the mall with my friends, what's up?"

"Listen, Peter, I just got a call from Cindy Wellington at church. Something's happened."

"What's wrong, Mom? What is it?"

"It's about Mrs. Stroud. Her son was killed in a drunk driving accident tonight."

My gut dropped.

21

Mrs. Stroud wasn't at school the next week. It wasn't surprising, but it still felt strange going to class and her not being there. We had a substitute named Mr. Baxter who was fine, but Mrs. Stroud's absence hung heavy in the air.

Alexander had been driving home from a friend's house when a drunk driver crossed the line and slammed Alexander's car into a tree. The other driver lived, but Alexander was killed on impact.

I couldn't even think about what Mrs. Stroud was going through, the kind of pain she must be feeling. I wondered whether I should call her or send her some flowers. She'd helped me so much, but how could I help her now in this situation? *Could* she be helped?

My grandmother came to visit on Wednesday. She didn't say how long she'd be staying for, but I assumed she'd be there until my mom felt a little better.

That night, after my mom had gone up to get a shower, my grandmother and I stayed in the kitchen and washed dishes.

"So how have things been since your father left?" she asked, handing me a plate to dry.

I shrugged, "She's really upset all the time lately. Crying a lot."

"Well, that's to be expected." Her hands swirled around in the soapy water, pulling out a fork covered in suds. "How about with you?"

"I'm okay. It feels better now that he's gone."

"What does?"

"Just the house, being at home." This was true to a certain extent. It was easier not hearing them fight all the time, but Mom was always crying now and that wasn't a good alternative.

"That's good." I could see her look at me out of the corner of my eye.

I finished drying the plate and reached up to place it on the cabinet shelf to my left. I hoped having my grandmother around would help my mom feel better, but I wasn't sure if anything could really do that.

The next day, I had to go back to school in the afternoon to pick up a book I'd left. The hallways of the school were filled with shadows as I walked to my locker. I was never in the school after 3pm. It was a different world. My shoes echoed against the floor with every step. The smell of old textbooks lingered in the air. A soft murmur came from the tutoring center as I passed. It was nice like this.

My left behind textbook was waiting for me when I got to my locker. Slamming the door shut, I heard a soft gasp raise up in response. It came from down the hall. I moved towards the end of the hallway, looking in each room. The source of the noise was in the last room. Mrs. Stroud's classroom. She was sitting at her desk, leaning forward with one hand on her forehead. Sunlight shone in from the window next to her, framing her shoulders and head. I was knocking against the door before I realized that I wasn't sure what to say to her. She looked up, lifting her hand to wave me over.

"Come in." Her voice was soft and weak.

"I don't want to bother you."

"Please, you're not a bother. Come in and sit down." She gestured to the chair across from her desk. Her face became clearer as I approached her. She looked like she always did, make-up on and jewelry. As the light hit the side of her face, I could see that her eyes were a bit puffy and her whole face drooped slightly.

We sat in silence for a moment.

"I'm sorry." I finally said, my voice sounding loud in the silence of the room.

"For what?" she said, distantly, as if she wasn't aware of what she was saying.

"For what happened. For what you're going through. I don't really know what I'm supposed to say. Everything just sounds stupid in this kind of situation." I didn't meet her eyes. I should know what to say to her right now. She always knew what to say to me.

"Everything you're 'supposed to say' has already been said by other people." she replied, crossing her arms in front of her and staring down at the papers scattered across her desk. "Just say whatever you're thinking. I've always told you never to censor yourself. What I'm going through shouldn't stop that."

"Why are you here?"

"I didn't want to be at home." She didn't explain further, but it had to be painful walking around her house with all those pictures of Alexander, with his bedroom right down the hall. She had talked about him a lot in the time I'd known her. She was prouder of him than she was her husband.

We sat there in silence for a moment as she stared off at some invisible thing that hovered above the stapler. She had never been this quiet. Finally, she sat up and rubbed her hand across her mouth. She sighed heavily and looked up at me.

"I'm just so tired. I feel like I can't take a nap without someone coming by to bring a casserole or 'visit with me'" she said, lifting her hands in air quotes. "They all want to come see us and talk about it. I can't talk about it anymore."

"Couldn't you tell them you just want to be alone?"

"Oh, no. They have to come. It's part of the show."

"What show?"

"The grieving mother and father show. They're obsessed with it. Whenever . . . something like this happens, people have to come by and see how the parents are taking it. And I just can't do it anymore. I'm tired," she said, looking down. She gently ran her fingertips across her hand, tracing the lines and bumping slowly over the knuckles. "I keep having to put my face on for people."

"I don't understand."

She sat up and leaned across her desk. Her eyes met mine, "Listen, I want you to know the truth. I want you to see things the way that they are. It would kill me if you grew up to become a part of this sanitized bullshit of a society we're a part of, okay? People feel things. Ugly things. Life isn't always a pretty little movie scene. And it doesn't have to be. It can be very good, but it can also be very bad. I'm not telling you this to make you feel sad. I just don't want you to grow up being afraid to show how you really feel. People get so uncomfortable around real emotions. They can't handle seeing someone really cry or scream or lose themselves. Sometimes you have too though. Sometimes you have to cry or scream, sometimes you have to lose yourself, and that's not a bad thing. It doesn't have to mean you're ruined. It just means you're in life and you've reached a hard part. You'll get past it, but you might have to be a little sad for a while. There's nothing wrong with that. You just have to allow yourself to feel it. Don't be like me. Don't let them force you into hiding it. Promise me."

She stared at me waiting for a response. Her eyes bore into me, focusing. She had never said anything like that to me before and I didn't really know what to say. I understood her though. I had seen it in my mother whenever we went to church. She would act differently, like she was handling everything okay. I had always thought it was just so she seemed strong, but maybe this was the real reason. Maybe she didn't have any other choice.

"Ok." I replied, "I promise."

She sat back in her chair again and took a deep breath. I could see her falling back into how she was when I found her. Her face began to sag again and her body sort of slid down into the mold of her chair. She let her wrists hang over the ends of the chair arms.

A few moments of silence passed before I stood up, "I should probably get home."

"Okay. I'm glad I got to see you." She looked up at me from her chair and made an attempt to smile that didn't quite work. I smiled back at her before turning and leaving.

22

I began to receive my college letters over the next two weeks. Surprisingly, I was accepted to all six schools I had applied to. This included the one in Chicago.

The Vanderguild Institute was one of the top liberal arts schools in the country. Their Creative Writing program had been attended by most of the writers who were currently on the New York Times Bestsellers list. With the application, they'd asked for a twenty-page writing sample. I had sent in the first twenty pages of my novel. And they'd accepted me. I had been accepted into their writing program.

The tuition wasn't cheap, but fortunately I'd received a lot of grants and loans through financial aid and Mom said we would be able to cover the rest. She'd been excited when I'd told her and Grandma. The smile that had spread across her face was the first one I'd seen in months. She'd hugged me for a full minute before passing me off to Grandma so she could start cooking my favorite meal in celebration.

I felt really, really happy. Until I had gotten the letter in the mail, I hadn't realized how much I really wanted to go. I had applied in a give-it-a-shot moment and hadn't expected to get accepted. As soon as I saw the letter, sitting amongst the other five, I knew it was the only choice.

"Dude, that's awesome!" Theo said, a big toothy grin on his face.

I was walking with him, Mallory, and Ryan through the mall. We were going to stop by Kevin's job to say hey and bring him coffee. He'd been working most days the past two weeks and we had barely seen him for a minute. When he wasn't working, he was either at school or studying for the test. We offered to come over and help him study, but he always said it was too much of a distraction and that we should just go out without him. For the past couple nights, we'd been dropping by to cheer him up.

"Thanks," I replied. "I'm actually really excited about it. More than I thought I'd be."

"Of course you are." Mallory said, looking over at me from Theo's other side. She lifted a hand and ran it through her long, dark hair. "Now I just have to decide which school *I'm* going to commit to."

Mallory had been accepted to USC, Marquette University, and Duke. I wondered if she wished she was doing the same thing as me, going to school for what she loves to do.

"So should I avoid mentioning it in front of Kevin?" I asked. I'd been thinking about him since I'd calmed down from all the excitement. Part of me felt guilty about getting accepted, about not having to worry about the money part of the equation. I didn't want him to feel hurt hearing us all talk about our plans for next year.

"I don't know." Mallory replied, shrugging. "I think it's best to just not talk about it unless he brings it up."

"You don't want him to get discouraged before the test." Theo added.

I looked to my right at Ryan. He nodded.

Ryan was going to take a year off before he started college. His therapist and his parents both thought it would be best for him to take some time to work on himself before leaving home. Ryan agreed with them.

When we got to the shoe store, Kevin was behind the register. The store was empty except for him and one other employee who was helping a woman find shoes for her preschool-age son. The little boy was sitting on one of the benches, swinging his legs back and forth quickly.

We walked up to the counter where Kevin was standing. He looked up from his computer when we set the coffee cup in front of him. His eyes looked heavy, like he hadn't slept much the previous night. He smiled, but the energy wasn't in it.

"Hey, guys."

"Hey, how ya feelin'?" Mallory said, crossing her arms and using them to lean against the counter.

"I'm okay. I was up really late last night trying to study, so I didn't get much sleep." He lifted his hand and massaged the side of his neck. He looked exhausted.

"You know, man, I don't think it'll hurt you to take a night off from this and just relax a bit." Theo said, his voice friendly. "You're killin' yourself."

Kevin's eyes moved to Theo's face for just a moment before falling back down. "I can't mess this up. I have to pass and get that scholarship."

"But you look miserable." Ryan said.

Kevin turned to him, "I'm okay, buddy. I promise. I just gotta get through this test and then I can relax. Just a little bit longer."

I looked over at Mallory who was staring at Kevin. I could see her eyes moving across his face and wondered what she was thinking. Did she believe him? I wasn't sure I did.

"So, what have you guys been up to today?" Kevin asked, looking at each of us, an empty smile back on his face.

I spoke up first, "Nothing, we've just been hanging around."

23

Kevin, Mallory, and Ryan came with me to the funeral for Mrs. Stroud's son. It was held at our church. The shutters on the large windows were all open as we walked into the sanctuary. The sun shone in, washing everything over in a warm glow that didn't quite fit the circumstances. Mourners filled each pew, all facing the front of the room.

The casket sat at the head of the sanctuary. It was black, extravagant bouquets of white lilies framing it. The top half was open to reveal what once was Alexander Stroud. We didn't approach the front, but I could see that he was decorated in a formal black suit with his hands resting gently upon his stomach. His hair was combed into perfect position with not a single hair out of place. I had never seen him look like that before, so stiff and perfect. It didn't seem real.

As we took our seats in the back, I noticed Mrs. Stroud sitting on the front pew to the right. I hadn't seen her since our talk at school. They told us she wasn't coming back to work for the rest of the year.

She wasn't moving. Her body sat rigidly still as she stared blankly at a spot on the floor just in front of the casket. There was make-up on her face and not a single sign of tears. Just numbness. To her right sat her husband. His long black hair was combed perfectly around his strong face. He wasn't crying, but every few seconds he would press his closed fist to his mouth as though he were keeping something locked inside it.

The service began a few minutes later. I'd never been to a funeral before, but it seemed like a nice service. The pastor spoke about young lives and being taken too soon. He told us how God had used Alex as a light for his peers. Some of his friends got up and told stories about fun times they'd had and how great of a friend he had been. His grandfather spoke of a time when he'd taken him to a baseball game. They were the kinds of stories people told when someone died. Stories that were full of happy memories, but never quite gave an idea of what the person was really like. Alex's parents stayed in their pew at the front, watching silently.

Half-way through, I glanced over at Kevin and Mallory. Mallory was staring down at the little program they'd given us when we got there. She kept running her finger back and forth across Alexander's name slowly. I could see Kevin looking around him at the other attendees. He seemed to be specifically interested in an older couple that was sitting a few pews in front of us on the left side. They appeared to be watching the service like the rest of us, but every few seconds the woman would lean her face into her husband's shoulder. Her eyes would close, and she'd gently rub her forehead back and forth against the material of his shirt. To my right, Ryan sat motionless as he stared forward.

At the end of the service, people were allowed to come forward to say a "final goodbye." A few of Alexander's friends went forward, whispering softly and holding on to each other. Some older women went forward in groups of two and three. As they turned to leave, they would give Mrs. Stroud a soft pat on the shoulder and quietly tell her that they were praying for her. All the formalities.

I could see what Mrs. Stroud had been talking about. It all played out like a scene from a movie.

After most of the people had gone up, I saw Mrs. Stroud move. She leaned forward slightly, her husband turning to her and wrapping his arm around her shoulders. Ignoring it, she stood up and turned towards the casket. She moved forward slowly, staring down at her feet. Those of us that were still seated watched as she padded across the space between her pew and what was left of her son. When she was within two feet of the coffin she reached forward and placed a hand on the side. Her pace slowed for those final steps. I could see her sigh deeply as she continued to stare at her feet. She breathed in, out, and back in again. Her head lifted. Not a sound was heard in the room as we all sat, spectators to what was unfolding before us. Mrs. Stroud hovered above the unlit candle of her son before a high-pitched squeak was heard coming from her lips. Her husband moved swiftly to her side, but before he could get there, she had turned around to face us. Her mouth was a gape, face frozen as her eyes stared aimlessly outwards. She held on to the side of the casket behind her, pressing down in an attempt to stay upright. As Mr. Stroud came to her side, she let go. Her body fell forward, a wail stretching from her lips. The ground came at her hard, a heavy thud echoing through the room. Animalistic moans of agony bellowed out of her body. Sob after sob rose forth like smoke from a chimney. She clawed at the floor with her hands as if she were attempting to dig through it. Gasping, her lungs reached for air. Eventually she screamed out, a piercing screech that filled the room, and let herself sprawl across the floor. Her husband, who had been trying to comfort her through it all, laid down next her and rested his head on her back. His hand came up by his head and tenderly rubbed circles in the space between her shoulder blades. She continued to cry against the hard wood of the floor, tears pooling around her cheek. People stared at her as if she were an innocent man on death row, but she didn't seem to notice. Her face had finally come off.

I felt Ryan take my hand and squeeze it in his. Looking, I found tears in his eyes. Quiet sobs shook his body. His lower lip was sucked into his mouth as his aching eyes stared forward. I assumed he was crying for Mrs. Stroud, so I wiped some of his tears away with my thumb and whispered to him that she would be alright. His grip on my hand tightened. I followed his gaze over to the casket where Alexander's body still rested. I turned back to him and lifted his hand to my heart. He wasn't crying for Mrs. Stroud. He wasn't even crying for Alexander. Ryan was crying for himself.

24

After the funeral, I headed home. I wasn't in the mood to go out and since my grandma had gone back to her house for the night to get a couple things, I wanted to check in on Mom.

When I walked in the side door, my mom was in the kitchen. Her back was to the door as she sat leaned forward over the kitchen table. I couldn't see her face, but I could hear the soft sniffle of her nose. Her back rose and fell with every deep breath she took, the kind of breath that took every bit of your energy to get through.

I stepped forward and stood at her side, watching her hands squeezing a crumbled tissue, listening to the gentle shush it made as she clenched it. Her profile was silhouetted against the light from the streetlamps, just visible through the closed blinds. Her cheeks were red and splotchy, a quiver hanging off the end of her bottom lip. What could have happened? It had just been a few hours since I'd seen her last. What could have happened in that short time? After all she'd been through, what was left? I thought back to when I found her in this spot on the night she and my father decided to separate. She'd been crying, but not like this. This state she was in was the result of a certain level of crying. She had been sobbing.

I didn't know how to respond to this. It had never been this bad before and I didn't know what I was supposed to say. Part of me didn't want to say anything. Seeing her like this made me feel sick, angry at whatever had hurt her. I knew, though, what had hurt her. There was only one thing that could hurt her like this, only one person.

A sigh fell from her lips when I finally asked, "What did he do?"

"Nothing, Peter. I'll be okay. How was the funeral?" Her body didn't move as she spoke.

"What did he do?" I repeated.

She lifted the tissue to pat at her damp cheeks and sighed, "Your father has found someone."

"What do you mean?"

"Well," she leaned forward even more, resting her elbows on either side of the cream-colored placemat we'd had since I was little, "Your father seems to have gotten himself a girlfriend."I thought back to the dinner we had the week before, sitting awkwardly across from each other in a booth at Chili's. Had there been any signs? Had there been any indication that he hadn't been spending all his free time alone? He had shaved, something he had been neglecting for the past couple of weeks, but that didn't seem like a sign of a life outside the one he had with us.

Then I remembered: he didn't have one with us anymore.

"Her name is Zoe." Mom said, a brief, sharp laugh jumping from her lips. "Kind of sounds like a little girl's name to me, but apparently she's a couple of years older than him."

I watched the tips of her hair sway across her back as she pressed her nose to the inside of the balled-up tissue. The night she and my father had agreed to separate, I had hoped that would be the last time I would find her crying like this.

But life doesn't let you off that easy.

She turned around in her chair, her aching eyes staring into mine. Her face was red from all the crying and there were a couple of strands of hair stuck to her bottom lip as she spoke, "How do you feel about all this, Peter? Are you okay?"

"I-" my eyes moved across the dimly lit room, jumping from shadow to shadow, "I don't know. I'm okay."

Truthfully, I really didn't know. Like with the separation, I felt outside of it all. It was as if it were happening to a friend and didn't affect me. I could see it tearing apart my mother, even feel her sadness lingering in the air after she wasn't in a room anymore. Yet, for reasons I couldn't understand, I never felt it myself. I never felt the pain or anger everyone expected me to be experiencing. The only thing I felt was the regret that I couldn't help my mom not feel it herself.

As I glanced around the kitchen, I felt her eyes stay on me. I didn't want to meet them, didn't want to see the heartache inside them. "You're completely fine with everything that's happening?"

"I guess so, I mean, it's not like I'm gonna have to see her that much."

She sighed, looking off at some space next to my shoulder, "He said he wanted me to know because he might want you to meet her at some point."

Good luck with that, I thought.

"I suppose I should be glad that he told me about it first, that he didn't just spring it on you. He told me he wanted me to know because he knew I would get upset if I found out through you. Clearly, it doesn't make a difference." she said, gesturing toward her teary eyes. "I'm glad he did it this way, I am, but still . . ."

I saw her eyes move from my shoulder. They moved across the shadows of the room, just like mine had, slipping across the cabinets and countertops. Her gaze went further, possibly through time even, back to when things were a little easier, a time between fights when things were a little less broken. I thought back to when we moved into that house two years prior. We had spent an entire day setting up the kitchen, unpacking boxes filled with dishes wrapped in wash towels. We plugged in the old radio my father's parents had given him as a teenager and listened to a dumb top 40 station while we lined our new cabinets and stocked them full of plates and serving dishes. My parents hadn't had a fight in a few weeks and things seemed so peaceful, like maybe this new house was a restart. My mother's eyes bounced around the room as if she were seeing us all in this better time, each of us back in our places. She hovered there in that time for a few more seconds, her eyes freezing over as she slowly came back to herself.

"I just never thought he'd find someone so soon." Her voice came out like a whisper as her eyes hovered over the countertop next to me. "It's not that I didn't want him to find someone. I'm not a cruel person. If he couldn't find happiness with me than I certainly hope he can find it with someone else. I just . . . I never thought it would be this fast. I've felt so stuck since we split up, trying to figure what to do next or what my life is going to be like now and he's already creating another one with someone else. I never thought I was a prize for him, I'm certainly not a catch, but isn't twenty-one years of marriage something to grieve?"

She addressed this to the room as if the years of their time together were standing there, an audience to her pain. I reached up and loosened my tie.

"I was just getting to a point where I thought I could breathe again," she continued. "It's like I've been through one of those old washing boards. I've been run back and forth and back and forth, and I was finally put up on the line. And now, just when I was almost dry, they pulled me down and started over again. I just want to be done." Tears were in her eyes as she begged this from the room. Her hands were held up as she waited for some kind of reprieve from her suffering. Silence came back at her, a silence I couldn't find the right words to fill. She lowered her hands and looked down at the thin, crumpled tissue in her hand, "I'm tired."

"You should try getting some sleep," I said, the only form of peace I could give her. This pain, this new form of rejection, seemed to hurt her worse than the separation. This helplessness that I felt over not being able to relieve some of the pain from her certainly did. I wanted to hit something, throw something, punch the fucking wall as I stood there unable to find the words that would help her breathe, that would help her live again.

"Yeah," she replied, spreading the tissue out flat against her knee. She sat for a moment longer before rising to her feet, using the tabletop for support. Closing the gap between us, she wrapped her arms around me and squeezed with the little bit of strength left in her body. I tried to feel comfort in her hug, tried to give her comfort, but I felt neither.

"I love you, Peter. I'm so sorry things are messed up right now. I'm sorry that I've let all my sadness fall onto you. It's not right. I wish you didn't have to come home to this."

"It's okay, Mom. It's not your fault. I love you too."

We stood there for a moment, holding each other tightly in the dark. When she finally let go, she walked over to the fridge, poured herself a glass of water and shuffled out of the room. I listened to her footsteps creeping up the staircase, headed towards what would be another restless night for us both. Standing there in the dark, I listened as she reached the top and padded down the hallway to her room. She had left a tear-stained circle in my t-shirt. I listened to my own deep breath in the silence, the cold circle pressed against my shoulder.

25

Over the next few weeks, things got worse at home. My mom began staying in bed all the time when she wasn't at work, only coming out for meals. Her cheeks seemed permanently tear-stained, red splotches spread out across her face.

Whenever her friends called, wanting to take her out to help cheer her up, she would tell them she had projects around the house she was trying to finish up. My grandma would try to encourage her to go out with them, to get out of the house for a while, but it never worked. She would just go back to bed.

My grandma kept up with the housework. I helped as much as I could, but when I got home from school she would have cleaned out all our kitchen cabinets or steam-cleaned the living room carpet. She was always moving. Occasionally, she would try to go into Mom's room and get her up, but she would just come out a few minutes later and shut the door.

Since Mom ate in her room, it was mostly Grandma and me at mealtimes.

"We have to get her up." I said one night as we sat over plates of lasagna.

She placed her hand over mine on the placemat and squeezed gently. "We will. Now is her time to grieve though. She has to work through some of this on her own."

"But I can help her." I replied, sitting back in my chair. "I can help her feel better. We just need to get her up and I can help her be happy again." And I could. It was my job to help her. She could be okay again.

She looked at me and her brow furrowed, mouth turning down. "Oh, Peter, that's not your job. That's too much for you to put on yourself. You're so young."

I hated hearing her say that. Yes, I was young, but that didn't mean I couldn't help her. I'd been there for everything, all the fights and silent treatments and painful words. I knew what happened when Mom felt hurt. I knew what movie to put on or food to make to help her perk up. This was something I could fix.

And my father. I hated him so much for all of this. Leaving was supposed to fix everything, not make it worse. How could he do this to her? To us?

When I went to bed, I lay there quietly and listened to my mom's sniffles through the wall and wondered how much longer she would have to grieve before she could get up again.

The night before Theo left town for basic training, we all went to a carnival in the next town over, Lowell. It was being put on by the high school there as a fundraiser for the football team. Mallory had heard about it through an aunt that lived there and thought it would be fun. We had been looking for a good way to spend Theo's last night and this seemed perfect.

Mallory picked us all up around six that evening. When they got to my house, I hopped in the back of the car with Kevin and Ryan. Theo was in the passenger seat up front with Mallory and seemed to be in a good mood. I had expected him to be acting differently than he normally did since it was his last night here, but he was in full swing. He and Mallory were laughing about something as I buckled up and we headed off.

As we pulled onto the highway, I began to think about the fact that I really didn't know Theo at all. Yeah, we hung out sometimes when Mallory brought him along, but I didn't really *know* him the way I knew Mallory or Kevin or Ryan. I wondered if we would ever see him again. Would I ever get the *chance* to know him?

Next to me, Kevin was hunched over a Chemistry textbook. He would read a few lines of the chapter and then make a couple notes in the notebook that he had resting on his knee. He had been adamant about coming. We all knew that it wasn't about getting a night off, but instead being there for Mallory when she and Theo said goodbye.

"How's it going?" I asked, settling into my seat.

"They don't make this stuff simple, do they?" He asked with a sigh. "It's like they need it to be hard so the people who understand it will feel better about themselves."

I laughed, "I'm not good at it either, but I can try to help if you want me to. I could quiz you?"

"Thanks, but I'll be okay. I can become a Chemistry genius in a month, right?"

"Oh, yeah. Totally." I said with a smile as he hunched back over his book.

I looked over him at Ryan who was on his other side. He was looking out the window at the setting sun. I watched his face, his eyes so intently focused on the fading light. The muscles in his face seemed to relax as he stared out the window, his lips parting slightly as he bit the lower one gently. After a moment, he turned and saw me watching him. I smiled and the corners of his mouth turned up slightly. He looked down at his hands in his lap before turning back to the window.

We reached Lowell forty-five minutes later. The carnival was set up in the large parking lot of a shutdown department store. We parked along a side street and walked over. It was a pretty impressive set up for such a small town. There were numerous booths selling cotton candy, funnel cake, nachos, and other snacks. Loud games designed to take money without providing the promised teddy bear were scattered around as well. There was a bounce house and inflatable obstacle course for the kids which had lines about four to five families long. Skee-Ball, a ring toss, and a dart game were among several activities to choose from. There was even a dunk tank featuring a very well-muscled man in swim trunks and a white t-shirt. A girl was attempting to hit the target against the good-natured heckling of the people around her. After two tries, she finally hit it and the guy fell into the water. When he rose back up, he had his arms firmly at his sides, trying to hide his shivering from the crowd.

The soft breeze swept around us as we walked, kids and their parents running in various directions. Night had fallen and the carnival lights were glowing all around us. The screams and cheers and rock music blasting from the speakers that were placed around created a melody of fun and chaos. It was a beautiful night to be with the people I loved.

Kevin was attempting to loosen up as we walked through the carnival. He looked around himself at all the people and booths and I could see that his mind was still back in the textbook. He was working so hard to prepare himself for the test and he deserved a night out.

Mallory and Theo were ahead of us a few paces, laughing and pointing at different things. We stopped at one of the dart games so Theo could give it a try.

"I want that big ass bunny, Theo. If you don't win it, we're leaving." Mallory said to him in a faux-stern voice, pointing at a large bunny rabbit in pink overalls that was hanging from the top of the booth.

"Yes, madam. I shall not rest until you have been provided with all your stuffed, polyester needs." Theo replied, bowing down to her before turning and picking up the darts. In quick succession, he tossed all three darts at the balloons, not hitting one.

Next to me Ryan laughed, his whole face lighting up.

"Well, I guess we can leave now." Mallory said, turning around with a smile.

"No, no, no!" Theo grabbed her by the shoulder and turned her around. "You're getting the bunny. Hey, Kevin, you give it a try now."

Kevin laughed and rolled his eyes, "All right, but don't give me crap if I don't get it. These things are rigged."

"Oh, come on, you're just saying that to save your manhood." Mallory replied, winking at him.

Kevin stepped up to the booth, passed over a couple bucks and picked up the darts. His shoulders tensed as he raised his hand. One, two, three, each one landed.

"WHOOOO!" Theo cheered, slapping Kevin on the back. "There it is!"

I could see Kevin's shoulders relax as he turned around and smiled modestly. The booth attendant grabbed the bunny and handed it to Kevin. He tossed it at Mallory with a smile.

"Is her majesty happy now?" Theo asked.

"Oh, I'm simply jolly!" she replied, shaking the bunny in the air.

"Splendid! Shall we procure some sustenance?"

"I should say so! Onward!" Mallory pointed down the path between the booths, linking her arm through Theo's. As we walked, she turned back to Kevin who was next to me. She smiled and mouthed "thank you." He nodded and smiled back.

We ended up finding a circle of food stands that were next to some picnic tables. We all got hot dogs and nachos and crowded around one of the tables. We ate messily and laughed at the kids that were running past with mouths full of cotton candy and popsicle smears around their lips. Ryan sat next me and scarfed down three hot dogs as well as half a serving of nachos. We all laughed when he got up and came back with some cotton candy.

I had brought my camera and after Mallory finished eating, she picked it up and began snapping pictures of us. I smiled as she took one of Ryan and me. Everything felt good. We were having such a great time together that I kept forgetting about the fact that we wouldn't be seeing Theo again for a long time after the night was over. He acted as if he'd forgotten, too. His smile was almost permanent, his laugh constant. Nobody was acting somber or upset. We were all talking and joking, just like we always did. It seemed strange, but maybe that's what we needed that night. Maybe that's what *he* needed.

After we ate, we walked around for a little bit more, stopping to try unsuccessfully at a couple more of the games. When we reached the kids obstacle course again, the line was much shorter.

"Hey," Kevin said, tapping Ryan on the arm. "Let's do it. You wanna?"

Ryan looked at it and laughed, "Okay, sure."

We all stood to the side as they got in line. When they reached the front, they slipped off their shoes and tossed them in our direction. The attendant counted them down and they dove in. We walked along the course, watching as they dove under beams and climbed over slides. Simultaneously, we all started cheering for Ryan, laughing as Kevin suddenly stopped and looked at us before busting out laughing.

"Come on, Ryan!"

"Go, go, go!"

"Kick his ass, Ryan!"

We continued cheering as they reached the end, Ryan falling through the hole first, followed by Kevin. They landed in a heap outside of the course and Ryan began laughing harder than I'd ever seen him laugh before. His face turned red and he held his hand to his stomach as his whole body shook with laughter. Kevin saw it and began laughing as well, bending down to rest his forehead on Ryan's shoulder. We all stood there laughing as more kids piled out of the hole, looking at us with weird faces.

Ryan slowly stopped laughing, breathing deep as he got up off the ground with a smile on his face. He and Kevin took their shoes and slipped them back on their feet.

"Good job, Ryan. I knew you would win." Mallory said, patting him on the back.

"I was clearly on a solo team in there. You guys all turned against me at the last minute in favor of this guy." Kevin bumped Ryan with his shoulder and they both laughed again.

"Whoa, I was totally cheering for you. You didn't see my 'Go Kevin!' poster?" I replied, holding my arms out like I'd been wrongly accused.

"I must have missed it somehow." he said with a smirk as he finished lacing up his shoes.

"All right, losers, I have to pee. Hold my bunny." Mallory tossed her bunny at Theo and ran a few yards away to a port-o-potty. She nudged the door open with her elbow and stepped daintily inside, pulling the door shut behind her. The three of us stepped over to one of the food stands and leaned against the side of it while we waited. I watched Theo look around at all the people, his eyes darting around the area. He breathed a deep sigh.

"I'm gonna miss all this."

"Maybe when you come back to visit we can do something like this again, all together. We could go to Six Flags or something." I replied.

"I'd like that," he said, turning to me.

I watched him for a moment, "Do you mind if I ask you something?"

"Sure."

"Are you scared at all?" I asked. Out of the corner of my eye, I could see Kevin and Ryan turn to see his response.

He was silent for a moment before answering slowly, "I don't think I'm scared about what I'm going in to. I think I'm scared that it's not actually what I'm supposed to do with my life."

"What do you mean?" Ryan asked.

Theo turned toward us, leaning his shoulder against the stand. "I've spent most of my teenage years preparing for this. For a long time, it's been my main focus, it's been the goal. I've always felt like this was what I was supposed to be doing. Now that I'm finally about to begin, I'm a little worried about what will happen if I was wrong."

"Why would you have been wrong?" I looked up at him, his eyes on the ground.

"That's the thing. I don't know. I don't necessarily feel like I'm wrong. It stills feels right. I'm just a little worried about what will happen if I've been mistaken this whole time. What would I do then?" He lifted his eyes off the ground to look at me.

"I don't know. I guess you have to just trust that you're not wrong. You've put so much of yourself into this, I don't know how you could be wrong."

"Yeah, I guess you're right." He lifted a hand to rub the back of his neck.

We stood there in silence for a moment before Ryan spoke up, "I don't think God would put you on that path if there wasn't a point to it. Even if this doesn't lead you where you think it will, I'm sure where you end up will be even better."

We all turned to Ryan who was looking at Theo. When he saw us turn, his face went red, and he looked down at his feet awkwardly. Ryan rarely said more than a few words at a time and when he did it was usually when someone spoke to him first.

"Thanks, Ryan. I'll try to remember that." Theo said, looking at him with a smile.

At that moment, Mallory came out of the port-o-potty wiping her hands on her jeans.

"What's going on?" she asked, looking around at all of us.

"Nothing," Theo replied, "We were just chatting."

The music stopped and a loud, perky voice came over the speakers to announce that the carnival would be shutting down in thirty minutes. Mallory's shoulders fell. It was almost time. Theo saw this.

"Hey!" he said loudly, making us all, including Mallory, look up at him. "Last person to the car has to ride home naked!"

He took off through the carnival and Mallory laughed, running after him. We all ran past the stands and booths and games, kids screaming in our ears and parents yelling after them. The purple, orange, and blue lights mixed together as we ran, creating a magical swirl of light leading us along. Darting around people, I turned to look at Kevin and Ryan who were running along beside me. They were both smiling and laughing, jumping past a couple middle schoolers. I could hear Mallory screaming out Theo's name and laughing as he reached back and grabbed her hand to pull her along. We ran out of the carnival exit and down the street to where we parked. We all piled into the car, laughing as we pulled off down the road.

We talked most of the way home, the car filled with constant noise. Somewhere around the city limits, it stopped, our conversation fading out like the end of a song. We drove in silence through the empty Haverty streets. The twenty-four-hour McDonalds stood bright and solitary amongst all the other dark restaurants and store fronts. To my right, Ryan sat still, the only movements being the gentle rubbing of his fingertips against his denim covered knees. On my left, Kevin sat with his hands joined in his lap, eyes trained on the back of Mallory's head-rest as she drove toward Theo's house at a speed just lower than the limit. From what I could see of Theo, his head was tilted down, his chin almost to his chest. His left leg bounced slightly. We all knew what was coming, but none of us knew what to say.

It occurred to me as we pulled up outside Theo's house that I had never actually seen where he lived. It was large and classic, white with blue shutters and a red door. There was a gold encased porch light that lit up the front steps. Even in the dim light from the streetlamp I could see that the flower beds were tended to recently. It was exactly the kind of house I would have imagined for Theo. It was exactly how Theo presented himself: clean and neat, well put together. Of course Theo would live in a house that was just as physically organized as he was.

The silence became uncomfortable as Mallory shifted into park, her headlights illuminating the stretch of the street in front of Theo's house like they were exposing something. Mallory let her hands fall to her lap from the steering wheel, her head turning to look out the driver side window. No one else moved. I watched Theo's shoulders rise and fall as he took in a deep breath. He turned toward his house, away from Mallory.

"Hey, uh," I said, breaking the silence as I leaned forward between the front seats. "It's been really great hanging out with you these past few months. I'm . . . I'm gonna be praying for you while you're gone. I hope you'll give me a call when you come back to visit. I'm really gonna miss you."

He turned back to look at me and for just a moment I thought he might cry. His hand came up and took mine and held it, not in a shake or in a firm way. He just . . . held it. Before letting go of my hand, he gave it a gentle squeeze. He didn't need to say anything back.

Theo turned around in his seat to look at Ryan, "Man, it's been really fun. You should . . . you should talk more. I like what you have to say. Don't silence yourself."

Ryan smiled and even in the dim light of the car I could see his cheeks going crimson.

Theo then turned to Kevin, "Kevin, I- "

"I'm sorry." Kevin's eyes finally moved from the back of Mallory's headrest and fell to his hands in his lap. "I'm sorry."

Theo just looked back at him, "Don't be."

Kevin looked up at Theo and, for what seemed like the first time since they'd met, I saw their eyes meet. They just looked at each other, Kevin no longer angry and Theo no longer trying to prove himself. For the first time, it seemed like they were finally seeing each other. The thought occurred to me then that maybe under different circumstances they could have been friends. They could have been good friends.

Theo turned to Mallory and placed a hand on her arm. She didn't turn from the window. A sigh fell from Theo's lips.

"It's time."

Without looking at him, she opened her door and got out. She passed in front of the car, the headlights shining through strands of dark hair, and stepped into the front yard. Mallory walked straight across the yard without stopping until she reached the top of the steps. She stood in the light of the porch lamp, her hands on her hips and her head down.

For the last time, Theo looked back at us and said, "Goodbye, guys."

We watched as he got out of the car and walked slowly across the yard and up the steps to where Mallory waited. Silence filled the car once more as their silhouettes fidgeted, the movements of their lips just barely visible. Mallory's hands stayed on her hips, her head turning from the ground to the door to the car.

I looked at Kevin. His eyes were focused back on Mallory, squinting in the dark. He was leaning forward and down slightly in what looked like an attempt to see her better. His shoulders were tensed.

Finally, after what seemed like minutes, Mallory lifted her hands from her hips and stepped forward to wrap them around Theo. It wasn't a long hug, but the way they held each other somehow felt final. It was as if they both sighed as they slowly parted again. Only a few more words were exchanged before Theo opened the front door, taking one last look at Mallory before closing it behind him.

As soon as Theo's door was closed, Kevin was opening his own and stepping out on the street. He walked around to the front of the car and stopped. Mallory turned from Theo's door and walked down the steps and into the yard. Her steps were slow at first, quickly speeding up as she got further into the yard. By the time she reached Kevin she was practically at a run. As she stepped off the curb, she fell into his arms. Kevin wrapped both arms around her body and pulled her in close. Her face was pressed against his, chin resting against his shoulder. Her legs looked limp beneath her. It was as if Kevin was holding her up, allowing her to take solace in the comfort of his arms.

Ryan and I watched them from the back seat of the car. Seeing this embrace made me realize how seldom it was that they hugged. They rarely even touched at all. Maybe it was too hard. Maybe touching, even in the most platonic of ways, just hurt too much. That didn't matter now. Kevin was comforting her in the best way he could, not with words, but with himself.

I looked at them and thought about their relationship. They looked out for each other, took care of each other on such a deep level and yet there was still so much distance between them. It was a distance they put there themselves, never allowing each other within arm's length. Looking at them and thinking about how they could never seem to get close enough to each other made me think about my mom. She had the opposite problem. My mom just wanted to get as far away from my father, and the way he made her feel, as possible. With that thought in my head, I couldn't see why they were holding themselves so far away from each other. I understood why Kevin was apprehensive, I even admired him for putting her above himself, but it just seemed like they would both be so much happier if they just gave in to it. My mom was heartbroken, and they had all this happiness just waiting at their fingertips. They were choosing to be unhappy. They were choosing to stay this way.

Next to me, Ryan looked down at his hands. He ran his left index finger slowly over the edge of the nails on his other hand. His shoulders were low and I could see a small frown on his lips. He seemed so weighed down now compared to how he'd been at the carnival. I didn't want him to worry about Kevin and Mallory, I didn't want him to let their unhappiness bring him down. I lifted my right hand slowly and placed it over his. He froze for a moment, his fingers coming to a stop. I watched him stare down at my hand over his, silent. After a moment, his hands separated, but instead of pulling away from mine, he lifted them, so my hand fell between his. His hands closed around mine and held it, his thumbs running over the space between my thumb and index finger. He didn't say a word or look up at me. He just watched my hand in his.

A moment later, the driver and passenger side doors opened. Mallory and Kevin got in and buckled up. They didn't say a word or look at each other as Mallory put the car in gear and pulled away from the curb. None of us said a word as Mallory dropped us off at our homes. Kevin looked at her once before shutting his door behind him when we stopped outside his apartment building. Ryan held my hand all the way to my house. When I went to let go, there was a second of resistance before his hands parted to free mine. He looked up at me as I stepped out of the car and I waved and mouthed "Bye." As I shut the door, I could see a small smile appear on his lips. "Bye," he mouthed back.

26

"His mom said he got there okay."

Mallory, Ryan, and I were stretched out on a blanket in my back-yard. Kevin picked up an extra shift at work, so we decided to spend Thursday afternoon at my place. It was warm outside for the beginning of April, a soft breeze slipping between the blades of grass around our heads. Every now and then the edges of the blanket would get caught up too, lifting around our bodies like the entire thing was going to carry us away.

I looked to my right, across Ryan who lay between us, to where Mallory was staring at the sky. One arm was behind her head, the other playing with the silver chain around her neck. The heart that hung at its center was pressed between her fingers.

She'd been distant since Theo had left on Sunday. I'd talked to or seen her every day that week, but our conversations didn't go as deep as they used to. They just floated on the surface, not quit dipping beneath the water. We would talk about school or trivial things like movies or music. Many times she would just sit and read or watch us play chess while Kevin, Ryan, and I talked. She would try to act as cheerfully quick-witted as always, but after a while the effort would wear on her and she'd settle, still contributing, only without the infectious energy. She'd try to blow it off, saying she was tired or stressed about something at school. It was her mission to not let it show just how much she missed him.

Whether she meant to or not, Mallory had fallen for him. All the talk about keeping her distance had been just that, talk. It wasn't as though she had intended for it to happen. That was just the way life seemed to be. It took over whatever plans you had and rewrote them, leaving the old ones blowing in the wind.

"That's good," I replied, "Did his mom say anything else?" Theo hadn't called Mallory since he'd left. She'd been getting all her information from his mom. I couldn't tell if this made things easier for her or harder.

"Nope." Her tone was careless, as if I were asking about her next-door neighbor, as she leaned up to run her fingers through her hair. She stretched her arms above her head as she laid back down. I watched her chest rise and fall, as if her body were mustering the energy to move past this point in the conversation.

"Have you measured for your tux, Ryan?" she asked.

"Yep." His eyes squinted in the sunlight as he stared up at the clouds, "I'm picking it up next Friday."

"Good. Kevin's getting his done tomorrow after school. My parents want to get us a limo because, you know, traditions. When is East Haverty's prom, Peter?"

"Weekend after yours."

"Going?"

"Hadn't planned on it."

"Come to ours."

The thought of going to prom seemed moronic. I had absolutely no desire to go stand in the corner of a room full of people sweating in terrible clothing and grinding all over each other. I had listened to prom talk for four years now and was, frankly, tired of it. As someone who didn't drink or grind, it seemed unbearably boring. Maybe, just maybe, it might be a little more bearable with some friends. "Sure, okay."

Next to me, a smile spread across Ryan's face.

"Perfect!" Mallory exclaimed, energy back in full force. She got up from the blanket and wiped her hands on her pants, "All right, I gotta head home. My grandparents are coming over for dinner. Do you need a ride home, Ryan?"

Ryan started to get up.

"I could take you home later," I said, rising up onto my elbows, "If you wanted to stay." I hoped he would stay.

He stopped in the middle of getting up, kneeling on the blanket. His eyes moved from the blanket to Mallory's knees before slowly rising to her face, "I'm gonna stay."

Mallory watched him lay back down next to me on the blanket, "Okay." She looked at me and winked before heading toward the house, "Bye, fellas!"

We laid there in silence, listening to Mallory enter the house, say goodbye to my mother and thank her for letting her come over, the distant click of the front door, Mallory's car starting, and the gentle purr of it taking off down the street.

I looked over at Ryan. His eyes were closed as he lay there in the sunlight. I turned on my side toward him and watched him for a few moments. One hand rested softly atop his belly while the other was stretched out at his side between us. His fingers ran lazy circles into the blanket, brushing over every thread and fiber. A breeze picked up and I saw his nostrils flare. His hair rustled gently, and it was beautiful.

My camera, which I'd brought out and forgotten, sat at the edge of the blanket. I quietly picked it up, bringing it to my eye and focusing. I watched him through the view finder, staring at his profile, the shape of his face. His eyes opened right as I pressed the shutter.

"Sorry," I said, laughing a little as I lowered the camera.

His eyes moved over my face slowly, a smile playing at his lips, "It's okay."

I set the camera back at the edge of the blanket and laid down on my arm. Ryan turned on his side toward me, hand coming up to play with a loose thread by his face. We were quiet for a few minutes, just him picking at the blanket and me watching him.

"I like spring.", his lips sliding together softly around the last word.

"Me too."

Silence. I watched his eyes, saw the change in them as it happened, as some kind of shift took place within him.

"I don't like Mallory being sad."

"Me neither," I said.

More silence.

"I hate seeing other people being sad."

"I do too." I replied, watching his eyes fall to the blanket. Maybe Ryan and I were more similar than I realized. We both saw the sadness in others. I thought about my mom, somewhere in the house. She'd been doing laundry with my grandma, a rare moment out of bed. I could see her in my head, carrying a laundry basket, that hopeless sorrow in her face.

My mind went to Brooke.

Brooke.

"Can I show you something secret?" I asked, getting up from the blanket.

He watched me for a moment before standing and following me into the house.

Ryan ran his fingertips across the wall, tracing the letters and words. He sat on the floor in the doorway of my closet, legs stretched out in front of him, inches away from mine as I sat, leaning against the end of my bed across from the closet, watching him.

I wasn't sure why I'd decided to show him the wall when I'd never shown it to my own parents, even though it wouldn't matter if they knew. It would just be words on a wall. Maybe I just wanted to show someone else. I had kept it a secret for two years, hiding it behind hanging shirts and ironed pants. Maybe I felt like I'd finally found someone I could show it to that would understand the way it made me feel. The sadness of the whole thing.

That was probably why. The sadness of it. Ryan knew that feeling. That sadness that came with life, with being a person. The sadness that Brooke probably felt when she wrote her little messages on the wall.

It was the weight of all the different struggles that life would throw at you. Despite not wanting to see that in others, he understood it in a way that felt familiar. We both understood the sadness in a way that connected us.

I could see it on his face. He smiled a little as he read each little feeling Brooke had left on the wall. It was the kind of smile that came about in conversation with someone. It was a smile that said, "I get that" and "I know what that feels like." It was the kind of smile that made you feel like you weren't alone. It made *me* feel like I wasn't alone.

"Sometimes I look at that when I'm feeling upset or lonely," I said. "I read them and imagine what she was going through or who she was talking about. It helps get my mind off things."

He turned to me. That smile. *I get that.* "What kind of things do you have on your mind when you come in here?"

"I don't know, just . . . stuff with my mom."

"Is she still hurting?"

"Yeah."

"How long has it been since they separated?" He leaned his head against the door frame.

"Four months, which, I mean, I know that's normal. I know divorce isn't something you just get over, but I . . ." In my head, I saw my mom crying at the kitchen table. "I'm just tired of watching her cry and not being able to do anything about it."

He looked down at his hands, clasped in front of him. His face fell slightly, the sides of his mouth turning down.

"What's wrong?"

He ran a thumb across the knuckles of his other hand. I watched his mouth open slightly, hesitating before speaking, "I was just thinking that's how I used to feel, kind of. Except I used to be your mom."

"What do you mean?"

He clenched his shaking hands together, "I used to get so sad, and it felt like there was nothing anyone could do about it."

My heart broke a little as he said that.

"Do you still feel like that?"

He took a deep breath and let go of his hands, "Not as much anymore."

It was at that moment that we both became aware of my hand on his calf. At some point while we were talking, I had dropped my hand to my side, where his ankles were, and was rubbing my fingers across the skin. I looked down, the contrast of his tan skin against the pale flesh of my hand was mesmerizing. The soft hairs slid back and forth between my fingertips. His warm muscles tightened and released beneath my hand.

I looked up at his face, his eyes watching my fingers move back and forth across his leg. There was something intimate about it, surprisingly so. Not sexual, necessarily, just intimate. Close. Closer than holding hands. It felt comfortable in a way that I'd never felt with anyone else.

It seemed like he could feel it, too. I could see it in his eyes as they watched my fingers slide across the skin of his leg. He looked apprehensive, but almost hypnotized at the same time. His own fingers were close together, one thumb running across the nail of the other.

Before I knew it, I was on my knees, crawling from my spot at the end of the bed to where he sat, no more than two feet away from me in the doorway of my closet. Sitting down, I turned toward him, my upper body facing his. His eyes were on my shirt. I lifted my hand, placing it on his cheek and turned his head. His eyes hovered over my lips, watching as I slid my tongue out to wet them. He was shaking slightly, but I knew it wasn't out of fear of me. He didn't let people get this close; he didn't let people touch him like this. I knew he wanted it though. I could see it in his eyes as he watched my lips, in his own lips as they parted to let out soft breaths, could feel it in his body and the magnetic pull that was drawing us closer.

I moved forward, head leaning into his. I paused, inches from his lips, listening to the heavy breath, feeling it against my lips. The scent of his skin floated under my nose.

I closed the gap between us.

A shudder went through his body as our lips touched. His were soft, smooth against mine. I ran my thumb across his cheek as I pressed myself further into the softness. It felt so good being that close to him, but I knew I couldn't push too fast. I had to make it okay for him. I had to make him feel like he could let go with me.

He pushed forward gently, restrained, as if he wasn't quite ready to let himself go off that cliff. His hand rested against my knee, his fist tight.

I let go of his lips, pressing my forehead against his. He wouldn't bring his eyes to mine, so I slid my hand around to the back of his neck, "Look at me. Please."

Slowly, slowly, he lifted his eyes up my face to lock with mine. In that moment, I had never felt closer to anyone.

"It's okay," I whispered into his fear.

I pressed my lips against his again. I felt his body unclench just a bit, testing the waters. His hand uncurled at my knee, not moving. He couldn't let go completely until he was sure. His lips pressed a little bit more into mine.

When it happened, I felt it. I felt his body drop into my arms, his lips pressing unrestrained into my own. His hand slid up my arm and wrapped tightly into my sleeve, pulling at me. He kept trying to get closer, his need coming out and grabbing me, anchoring itself on me. He was going over a cliff and needed me to catch him. So I did.

When I got home from school on Wednesday, my mom and grandma were cleaning out the attic. I found them at the bottom of the attic steps with large black trash bags. They were shoving a bunch of my baby toys into one.

"Hello, Grandson. How was school?" Grandma said as she tied up the top of the garbage bag and tossed it into a pile inside the doorway of my mom's room. Her red hair was tied in a bun at the back of her head.

"It was okay. Nothing exciting." I replied, watching my mom pull her hair back and fan at her neck with one hand. "What are you guys doing?"

"Your grandmother thinks we need to purge the house." Mom said, leaning down to get another trash bag from the roll, her hair hanging down around her face.

Grandma rolled her eyes, "We're not *purging* the house. I just thought a little spring cleaning would be good for your mother. It got her out of the bed!"

"Mom . . ." I watched my mother sigh and toss down the bag she was trying to open. "I'm having a really hard time right now."

"I know, sweetheart, but we can't let you stay in bed all day. You have to greet the world."

Mom turned away, placing her hands on her hips. Grandma looked at me and nodded for me to go on into my room.

Once inside, I shut the door and sat down on my bed to do homework. I could hear Mom and Grandma talking on the other side of the wall. It wasn't coming through clearly, mostly in mumbles and whispers. This time, I didn't try to hear through the wall. I went and sat down in my closet with my notebook.

I thought about sitting there with Ryan several days earlier, his warm breath against my lips. I wanted him there now. We hadn't hung out since then and I wanted to be close to him again. I had texted him the next morning to make sure he was okay with everything. He'd responded that he was happy and that he was excited to go to prom together.

I looked at Brooke's writings and felt strangely comforted by the fact that Ryan knew. It wasn't my secret anymore, but I had shared it with someone I could trust.

An hour later, when I got up from my closet floor to go to the kitchen, I opened my bedroom door to find my mother's shut.

"Is she in bed again?" I asked Grandma when I found her in the kitchen reading a book at the table while pasta sat on the stove, waiting to boil.

She looked up at me from her book, red hair shining in the overhead light. "Unfortunately, yes. I pushed too hard today." Sighing, she put the book down on the placemat in front of her. "I'm gonna make it happen, Peter. I'm gonna get your mother up. I promise."

I wanted to believe her. I wanted to believe that she could make Mom happy again. But lately, it felt like that just wasn't possible.

28

The prom at West Haverty was themed "Old Hollywood." Mallory was wearing the yellow sundress she had gotten at the mall that day after I'd first met them. The rest of us were in tuxes that didn't quite fit properly.

The night began with pictures. Kevin brought Ryan over to my house in his car and Mallory arrived a bit later in the limo her parents had gotten for us. As soon as we were all together, my mom proceeded to fill up her camera memory card with photos of me, photos of Ryan and me, photos of Kevin and Mallory, photos of just Mallory, and finally ten group shots.

"We need to go, Mom."

"It's your only prom! Shut up and let me take some pictures."

It was the first time in three days that she had any energy at all, so I stopped protesting. My grandma went from smiling at me to smiling at Mom and back.

From my house we hopped in the limo and went to Kevin's. I had never been in a limo before, but it wasn't as exciting as I thought it would be. I mean, it was nice, but it just didn't have that glamorous appeal like in the movies.

When we got to Kevin and Jeremy's apartment, Jeremy took all of eight photos before telling us to "get the hell out and go have some fun." We went on to Ryan's house from there. I had never met his parents before, but they were immediately kind and welcoming. His mother looked several years older than mine with blonde hair pulled back in a clip and worry lines. His father looked a couple years older than her, clad in jeans and a Cubs shirt, his walk relaxed and easy. They both shook my hand a little longer than they shook Kevin's and Mallory's.

"It's so wonderful to meet you." His mother said as she let go of my hand, bringing hers back to grip her other one in front of her waist.

His father patted me on the shoulder, "We're real glad Ryan has you in his life, son. You're a good man."

Ryan's parents seemed so kind and yet I could see what he had mentioned at the bowling alley about feeling watched all the time. They both appeared slightly cautious, watching him closely as we took pictures together and talked. Ryan looked exactly like them. He shared his father's kind eyes and when his mother smiled it was the same small smile that he had given me so many times. They were wonderful people who looked at their son with so much love and care. I felt comfort in knowing that he had this to come home to when he wasn't with us.

As we all stood in the front yard, Ryan looked at me in the dimming sunlight. I could see him blush slightly. Seeing them now, standing in the front yard, his father putting an arm around his son's shoulders and Ryan leaning into it slightly, they looked so whole. They fit together so well in their roles. I was happy that Ryan had that, but it made me wonder what it was like. It seemed so nice, so comfortable. What did it feel like to have a family that was so complete?

We got a few pictures there before hopping back in the limo. Mr. and Mrs. Diaz were celebrating their wedding anniversary that night. Mallory had told them that she would get some of my mom's pictures for them so they could make their dinner reservations. So, with the pictures done, we headed to the school.

I had never been inside West Haverty High School, but it didn't seem that different from East Haverty. All the high school essentials were still there, only in the West Haverty colors of red and navy blue. It wasn't nicer than our school. It was just another school.

We entered through the main door and walked down a couple different hallways before we got to the gym. A gold and white balloon archway had been created to stand above the doorway. A teacher wearing a white button down and a loose red tie sat at a table taking tickets. Mallory handed him ours and we stepped inside.

The gym was simultaneously dark and bright. Big white spotlights were perched atop high stands around the edge, pointing down on a mass body of students. Most of the girls were dressed in big, sparkly dresses and dancing with boys in tuxes that were much nicer than ours. Tables with gold-colored tablecloths made a big U around the room, framing the dance floor. The centerpieces at each table were giant film reels. At the top of the U was a big soundboard being manned by an audio engineer who kind of looked like Ryan Seacrest. On either side of the sound board were two giant statues made to look like Academy Awards. In the corner to the left of the door was a table with a giant bowl of punch. We headed there first. Punch in hand, we found an empty table and sat down. A loud rap song blared from speakers around us.

"Oh my gosh, I feel like my eyeballs are vibrating!" Mallory called out over the noise.

"I think that's how they're supposed to feel!" Kevin yelled back.

"Should we dance?!"

"Sure!"

Leaving their cups at the table, they moved out into the writhing bunch. Most of the people dancing were just grinding against each other in a rhythmic motion. I watched as Kevin and Mallory began doing the twist next to a couple that might as well have just gone to a hotel.

I turned to Ryan who was sitting next to me, sipping his punch. He looked so cute in his tuxedo. I hadn't really had a chance to look at him since he had gotten to my house because of all the pictures, but sitting there now I could finally see how handsome he looked.

It was interesting how easy our relationship had shifted since the kiss in my room. We had just fallen into something together. He had come over Thursday night and we had done homework on the floor and watched a movie. The only difference was that I could kiss him now, I could hold him. God, I loved holding him. And he would want me too. We laid on the couch and he slid up close next to me and laid his head on my shoulder. Just like that. It had been so simple. There was never any conversation about us being together. We just were. Kevin and Mallory didn't mention it either. We had all met up for coffee Friday night. Ryan and I were holding hands when we walked in and they just looked up at us and smiled, Mallory winking at me, before going straight into a conversation about football uniforms. Nobody blinked an eye. It almost seemed like it was inevitable, that we were always going to end up together.

He set his cup down on the table and looked up at me. I took his hand, rubbing my thumb over the skin on the top. He squeezed mine.

"Do you wanna dance?" I asked as a slower song came over the speakers.

He nodded and we stood up. Leading him on to the dance floor, we took our place in the crowd. I put my arms around him and he slid his hands up my back, leaning his head against my shoulder. We swayed there, holding each other as a soft melody surrounded us. I closed my eyes, not looking at the couples around me, just feeling the boy in my arms. I had imagined this, this very moment. In the movies, the couples were always dancing together just like this at their prom. I had always wondered what it would be like, wondered if it would be as nice as it seemed. It was. I wrapped my arms around him tighter, turning my head so I could smell the scent of his shampoo, a scent I had gotten use to so quickly on Thursday night. This was what I had wanted for so long. I had wanted a moment like this, a moment with someone. And it was better than I thought it would be. It was better because it was with him. We stepped and turned and swayed and I prayed that the song wouldn't end, that it would just last forever so I could stand there with him in my arms and feel this with him.

"Hey," I whispered into his ear.

He leaned his head back from my shoulder and looked up into my eyes with those beautiful blues.

"I'm glad you're here. I'm glad it's you." I whispered so only he could hear.

That sweet smile came alive on his face and he said, "I'm glad it's you, too."

I leaned my forehead down against his and we stood there, standing still in the moving crowd, just looking into each other's eyes. I felt every beat of my heart and, I imagined, every beat of his.

The song slowly faded out and was replaced by a Katy Perry hit. We laughed as the people around us began shaking their asses again. As we stepped back over to the table, Kevin and Mallory found us.

"This is boring." Mallory said, looking around the room.

"Yeah, let's get outta here. We can have more fun somewhere else." Kevin added.

I looked at Ryan and he nodded like he was ready for whatever would come next. I took his hand again and we all ran for the door, sprinting down the hallway and through the front door to the school.

We got back in the limo and had the driver take us back to my house where we piled into Kevin's car. For a while we just drove around with the windows down and the music up. I took off my tie and leaned my head out the window, feeling the breeze blowing through my hair. Ryan sat next to me, his own tie hanging loosely from his neck. His head was leaned back against the seat and his eyes were closed, peace on his face. I leaned over and kissed him on the cheek, my hand coming up to tickle him under his chin. He laughed and flinched away from me.

Kevin went through a McDonald's drive thru and we all got burgers. Parking out at Manchester Park, we sat on the bumper of his car and ate. Mallory started talking about a girl she'd seen at the dance who was "practically sucking her boyfriend's tongue out of his mouth" and how his jaw was "drenched with lipstick and saliva." Kevin squirted ketchup onto his hand and rubbed it against his cheek before pressing the side of his face against Mallory's.

"IS THIS SEXY???" he screamed.

She squealed and jumped off the bumper, running out into the park. He chased after her with Ryan and me in tow. We all ran through the park, screaming and hollering out. The air blew around us and it felt like we were flying, soaring through the park together. We ran around the trees and jumped across the paths that wound their way through the park. Eventually we landed in a clearing, the trees separating to let the moonlight shine through. The running caught up with us and we all sprawled out on the grass, laughing, and breathing heavy. I looked up at the moon, trying to calm my racing heart. Looking to my left, I could see Ryan doing the same. On his other side, Kevin was sitting cross-legged, leaning back on his hands. There was still a smear of ketchup shining on his cheek in the moonlight. Mallory was on my right, running her hand across her sweaty forehead. We laid there in silence for a few minutes, the sound of crickets in the air.

"I don't want to go to school on Monday. I don't want to study. I don't want to go to work." Kevin said, looking up at the sky. "I just want to stay here, like this. I just want this."

"Me too," I replied, looking at him. He looked so much more tired suddenly. His shoulders looked slack as he leaned against his hands. His mouth hung open slightly, his eyes hooded. I watched his chest rise and fall.

"I just want it to feel easy like this for a little while longer."

"It can, tonight." I said and he looked at me and smiled.

At that moment, a soft gasp came from Mallory. I turned to see her laying down on the grass with a hand at her chest. Shiny tears were slipping out of the corners of her eyes, escaping into her hair. Her stomach shook slightly as the tears fell. I looked at her eyes, wide and distant. Soft breaths came from her parted lips. Turning to Kevin, he looked at me with a frown. Ryan leaned up on his elbows and watched her, his eyes soft.

"I don't want to go to school in the fall," she let slip out.

A soft whimper fell from her lips as she continued to cry. I reached across the grass between us and took her hand, holding it tightly within mine. She gripped my hand back. Ryan got up and crawled around to her other side and laid down next to her, putting his arm around her waist and his head against hers. Kevin didn't move for a few moments, but finally got up and went to sit above her head. His hand came down and brushed her hair back from her wet cheeks. She closed her eyes and laid there for a while, crying in the moonlight surrounded by the people who loved her.

29

The next time I went to dinner with my father, we went to Pizza Hut. It was a nice change in that the buffet allowed me a chance to get away from the table for a moment, to have just a few minutes where I didn't have to pretend everything was fine. I would just get a slice at a time so that I would be able to go back more often.

It was hard to be nice to him. Every time I looked at him, all I could think about was him and his new girlfriend, him hurting Mom, and him choosing to move on from us so quickly. All I wanted to do was get up and leave.

"So how's school?" he asked, and I wondered if that was the only thing that popped into his head when he talked to me.

I took a sip of Coke, "It's fine."

"Your grades are okay?"

"Yep," I replied. "Always are." I could hear the frustration coming into my voice and I pushed it down. If he heard it, he pretended not to notice.

He ran a hand through his black hair, "Yeah, you've always been pretty smart. You're a lot smarter than me, that's for sure." Sighing, he took another bite of his pizza.

It was silent for several minutes and I searched for something to fill the gap. Part of me was annoyed with the fact that I was the one who was having to come up with a topic of conversation. I felt like I shouldn't have to be doing the talking for both of us. He was the parent who never got to see me. Shouldn't he be the one doing the talking, the one asking questions about what I've been up to? Shouldn't he be curious about my life? It just frustrated me, but what really got to me was how hard it all felt. Being around him felt like work. It was all too exhausting.

"How's everything with you?" I asked, lacking a more interesting conversation starter.

"Oh, you know, just getting by." he said, nodding his head gently. "Your Uncle Billy was in town last week visiting. He said to tell you hello."

More silence.

"How's your mother?"

Seriously?

"She's fine."

"Is she holding up okay?"

Holding up okay? How did he *think* she was doing? And why was he asking me this? He left. He didn't get to ask me shit like that.

"She's doing her best." The tension was rising in my voice again. I didn't push it down this time.

He looked down at his plate, "You know, I've been struggling with this too. It's been really strange to leave work and not go back to the house."

I didn't want to hear this. Why was he telling me this? I just wanted him to stop talking.

"My apartment is too quiet."

Anger was pooling in my stomach. I wanted to scream at him or yell at him to stop, to shut up, but I couldn't. I couldn't say anything. If I did, it would turn into some big conversation, or worse, it wouldn't.

"I miss- "

I pretended to look at my phone and grabbed my coat. "I'm sorry, I didn't realize what time it was. I told my friends I would meet them at 7. Thank you for dinner." I pulled my napkin from my lap and put it on the table.

"Peter, I just want you to know that I miss you guys."

"Than you shouldn't have left."

There it was, out before I could stop it. I looked at him, waiting for a response, waiting for him to say *anything*. He said nothing, just looked from me to the table to his hands in his lap.

"I, uh . . .." His mouth hung open awkwardly.

"I'm sorry. I have to go. Thank you again for dinner." I got up and walked out.

Once I was in my car and driving away, I finally realized what I said and what it meant. I had gone from hoping for a divorce to worrying about it and now I was almost wishing it had never happened. Nothing was how I had anticipated it being. My mother was a mess, and I didn't know what to do about it. Prior to splitting with my father, she at least had a small level of happiness in her life. She smiled and laughed, even if both went away when my father was around. Now, she just stayed in bed all day.

I didn't regret what I said to my father. If he missed us so much than he should never have left in the first place. He didn't get to sit there and talk about how hard things were for him now. He just didn't.

When I got home, I found my mother sitting on the couch looking through an old scrapbook.

"Hey," I said, sitting down beside her. "Which one is this?"

"Your preschool years," she said almost like a whisper. Her eyes were red like she'd been crying.

We sat there for several minutes, flipping through the pages. The book was filled with pictures of me in Halloween costumes and at preschool birthday parties. There was one where I was sitting in front of my own birthday cake, tears streaming down my cheeks, all while wearing a train conductors' hat. Another picture showed me standing between my parents as they knelt at my sides on my first day of preschool. The little two-year-old me was smiling up at the camera, happy as could be.

The scrapbook ended with a picture of me at my preschool graduation. We were all wearing little white caps and gowns as we stood in a row at the front of our church.

"You'll be graduating high school in just over a month," my mother said, running her hand across the page to clear the dust. "I don't know what I'll do in this house all by myself." The side of her mouth twitched, and I wondered if she was going to start crying again, but she didn't.

Closing the scrapbook, she stood up and walked over to place it on the bookshelf. Turning, she headed for the kitchen.

"Grandma ordered pizza. It should be here in an hour."

"Hey, Mom?" I stood up and walked over to her as she stopped and turned back to look at me.

"Even though I'm going to college, I'm still gonna be coming home and stuff. Besides, I'll just be in the city. I'll be close enough to come home on weekends and stuff." I watched her, hoping this would give her some kind of comfort.

She just raised her mouth in an attempt at a smile and said, "I know, son." Turning back, she walked into the kitchen.

Later that night, I sat in the bottom of my closet writing and thinking about the fall. I was working on a scene where Connor and Amber discussed what they would do if Amber had to leave town with her parents. Setting my notebook down, I thought about what my mother would do when *I* left. She was so broken and upset and I couldn't see it getting better. How would she be when I wasn't here to talk to her, to help cheer her up? I didn't want to think about her shuffling around the house all alone, no one to talk to or eat dinner with. I felt certain Grandma would stay with her until she was better, but when would that be?

Maybe I could stay home for a year, like Ryan. I could go to the Haverty Community College and take some courses. It might be smart to take some of my GenEd classes there to save money. That way I could be home to give Mom a little more time to get better, to be happy again.

I looked over at my wall, my eyes landing on Brooke's words:

You can be happy like this

30

I woke up to the sound of voices. Gray light shone in through the open blinds in my room, dark rain clouds visible just outside. Small raindrops were already scattered across the windowpane. The scent of freshly brewed coffee slipped under my closed door. My desk lamp was still on from where I'd been too lazy the night before to get up and turn it off before going to sleep. A pencil lay across my open notebook. I hadn't gotten much writing done the previous night; my head full of too many things.

My grandma's voice came through the thin walls. I could hear her just across the hall in my mom's room. She was frustrated.

"Come on, honey, it's time to get up. I'll make you some breakfast."

I stood up and quietly stepped over to the door, pulling it open just a couple of inches to see across the hall. My mom's door was open and I could see her bed, with her still in it. She was turned on her side and I couldn't see her face, but her red hair was spread out across the white pillowcase. My grandmother was standing at the side of the bed, looking down at her, with her hands on her hips. She was silent for a moment before crossing in front of the bed and disappearing from view. A second later, there was a *whoosh* of fabric and light spilled into the room. I heard my mother's muffled grunt into the pillow.

"I don't need to get up yet. It's my day off, just let me sleep." My mom said as she turned over in the bed, away from the window. Her face, now visible, pressed into the pillow as she reached down and pulled the blanket up a little more.

"Nope, you're getting up. You're not going to sleep all morning. I won't allow it. Come on, I'll make you some breakfast." My grandmother was back on the other side of the bed, looking down at my mother. Gray light from the window shone on her lavender sweater.

"Just let me sleep, Mom." I could hear in her voice that she was starting to get frustrated. "I'm tired. I've had a rough few weeks. I don't think there's anything wrong with me sleeping in on a Saturday morning."

"But it's not just today. You can't keep doing this. You have to get up and face the day. Now, come on and get out of the bed." She reached down and grabbed the blanket with both hands and pulled it down to the end of the bed. My mother sighed loudly and sat up. Her hair fell into her face and she lifted a hand to push it back behind her. She rubbed her eyes, pressing the fingertips of each hand to the bridge of her nose. Her face was splotchy from sleep.

My mother leaned her head down in her hands. "I've been through so much these past few months and I'm *tired.* I think, after everything with Saul, I deserve to sleep when I want to sleep." Her voice sounded groggy as she lifted her head. The light from the window hit her face and I could see her eyes glistening. "I'm tired, Mom. I'm just so tired and I don't want to do anything except sleep right now. Please, just let me rest."

She laid back down on the pillow, pulling the blanket with her. My grandmother stood there for a moment, hands on her hips. Slowly, she sat down on the edge of the bed and reached her arm out, placing it on my mother's shoulder. Her red hair hung down around her face.

"Do you want to know something?" Her voice was calm and soft as it came out. "You were very little when my mother died. You were still in preschool. She had been battling with cancer for a while and I used to leave you with your father after we put you to bed so I could go to the hospital to stay with her. Those few months when she was so sick and didn't leave the hospital, barely got out of the bed for weeks, were the hardest of my life. Every day that I woke up I felt like I had this dark cloud hovering over me." She lifted the pillow behind her, placing it against the headboard, and leaned back. Her hand stayed on my mother's shoulder as she continued. "My father was always full of optimism, and I usually took after him, but those months took a toll on me. When my mother finally went on to heaven, I felt like I couldn't breathe. I would wake up in the middle of the night gasping for air. There were many nights that your father stayed up with me, just rubbing my back until I fell asleep. For weeks, I wouldn't get out of bed until noon and then I would just sit around the house in my robe. I wouldn't do anything, not even play with you. It got to the point where I couldn't even pick you up without crying. It was the most painful and exhausting time in my life, and I thank God every day that I made it through." Her voice was deep and hollow.

I had never heard her talk about my great grandparents before now. They were always absent from her stories.

I heard my mother's voice, "How did you get through it?"

My grandmother's hand began moving in slow circles over my mother's shoulder. "My father. He came by one day and he laid in bed with me just like this and you know what he told me? He said to me, 'Evelyn, the hardest thing about waking up every day is facing the world. When times are hard like this, the bravest thing you can do is get out of bed in the morning.' He helped me. He would come over every day to have breakfast with me so that he knew I was getting up. Every day for a month. He did that for me while he was dealing with his own pain, his own loss. He wouldn't let me drown in mine and I'm not going to let you drown in yours. That's why you have to get up. You have to get out of this bed and face the day because one day your son might be in this same spot and you'll need to help him just like I'm helping you now. Now, come on." She swung her legs over the side and stood up. She wiped her fingers across the corners of her eyes and turned around. "I'm going downstairs to start making breakfast. I expect you down there in ten minutes."

I quickly shut my door so I wouldn't be seen. Leaning my head against the doorframe, I suddenly felt so thankful that my grandmother was there. If I had to go get her up, I wouldn't know what to say or do. My grandmother was so strong, so understanding. I wondered about the pain she felt when she lost her mother and if she still felt it now. Did she still have trouble getting up sometimes? Who helped her now that her father and husband were both dead? I couldn't imagine her being in my mother's position, struggling to just get out of bed every day.

Quietly, I stepped back over to my bed and got under the covers. I didn't want to go out there. I didn't want to go down to breakfast and see my mom so upset, to see my grandmother and think about when she was just like my mom. Turning over, I closed my eyes and pulled the blanket tighter around myself. My mother may have to be brave and face the day, but I wasn't ready yet.

The party was at the house of a guy named Mitch Carlson. It was a small house, one story with a big front yard. There were cars parked all long the curb of the street. The front door was open, light pouring out into the yard. Silhouetted teenagers passed back and forth in front of the doorway, casting long shadows across the lawn.

Kevin parked the car a few houses down and we all got out.

"How do you know this guy, again?" I asked them as we began walking down the sidewalk toward the house.

"He was on the soccer team with me," Kevin replied, running his hand through his black curls. "Mitch is a pretty good guy. He's way into the party scene, but he's still cool."

"He's cool to *you*," Mallory added. "He won't say two words to me. I think it's because I turned him down that one time he asked me out. What did he expect? I heard him telling his buddies that Cleo Rothdale sent him a topless pic to wack-off to. I was not going to put my money into that spank bank."

Ryan laughed.

Kevin stopped, "If you don't like him than why are we here?" He looked at her with heavy eyes.

"Because we're graduating in a couple weeks. We should go to at least *one* graduation party, even if it's just for the experience. Besides, maybe it'll be fun."

I turned to see Kevin look down at his feet as he began walking again.

"I could use some fun," he said, his voice heavy with exhaustion.

Kevin told us that the test was really hard. He said that there were about one hundred kids spread out through several classrooms taking the test. We had helped him study for the past several weeks and when Mallory asked if he thought it had helped, he said it had only helped to a certain extent. There had been questions that he still didn't know how to answer. When he had picked us up for the party, his entire face was downcast. Mallory said that we could just stay in if he wanted to since he was so tired, but he wanted to go on to the party.

When we got to the house, we could hear rap music playing. It didn't get loud until we reached the door and even then, it was just quiet enough to not warrant a neighborly call to the cops. As we stepped inside, the stinky odor of marijuana filled my nostrils. Right next to the door was a guy with long black hair and a joint in hand. He was just sitting there, smoking away with blank eyes. The door opened into a living room where a large group of people were congregated. On the other side of the room was a door that led to a kitchen. Just past the door was a hallway.

Several people sat on the couch, some in the laps of others. A hookah sat in the middle of a wooden coffee table, each of the four pipes being used by someone in the room and then passed. A couple of them looked up at us briefly, not giving us more than a glance before turning back to each other. Red Solo cups littered the floor, some with fluid running out to soak into the beige carpet. Across from the couch was a large TV with *Alien* playing on a big flat screen. A few, clearly drunk, guys sat directly in front of the TV with drooped eye lids and full cups in hand. A bag of chips was dumped upside down on the floor in front of them. I looked over at Mallory who was grimacing. Kevin just stepped past them and into the kitchen. Ryan took my hand.

The kitchen was a bit bigger than the living room. There was a large black table where another group of kids was playing a card game. Behind them was a big sliding glass door that led out onto a patio. I could see even more people outside. Across the room from the table was the kitchen. It was a typical kitchen, white cabinets with a brick backsplash. An island in the middle of the room was covered in various bottles, from soda to tequila, as well as more cups. People filled the kitchen, leaning against cabinets with their cups of booze, talking to friends. A couple was standing off to the side, close to the door that led to the living room. The guy had his hand on the girl's waist and was whispering something in her ear that was making her smile.

I hadn't been to a party since freshman year, but it didn't seem any different now. We were just older. It seemed like a strange way to have fun. I didn't understand what made this enjoyable, sitting around in a smelly room with a bunch of people you probably wouldn't see after graduation. What was the point?

Ryan moved in close to me, leaning his head against my shoulder.

"Are you okay?" I asked, turning to look at him.

He nodded.

"Are you sure? We can leave if you want to."

"I'm fine," he replied. "I just haven't been to a party in a long time."

"I'll be with you the whole time." I smiled at him. "We can leave at any point."

"Okay."

"KEVIN!"

I turned to see a short, stocky guy with blond hair looking our way. He stepped through the crowd from his place by the sink and ran up to Kevin, hugging him and giving him a hard pat on the back. He was wearing sweatpants and a tank top, his arms bulging at his sides.

"Hey, bro! You came! How's it going?" He smiled big, showing straight white teeth.

Kevin smiled, "Hey, Mitch. Yeah, I'm doing okay. We thought we'd come check it all out tonight."

"Nice, man, I'm glad you're here. Grab a cup and get yourself a drink. You guys, too!" He said, looking at each of us.

Kevin stepped forward and reached for a cup.

"Kevin?" Mallory began, stepping forward and putting a hand on his shoulder.

He turned around and looked at her, "You can drive us home." Turning back, he searched through the bottles before picking up one with a Smirnoff label.

I had never seen Kevin drink before then. I didn't know he drank period. Maybe it wasn't a problem, but the look on Mallory's face as she turned around made me feel nervous. Her lips were in a tight line and her hands were on her hips.

"Is everything okay?" I asked.

"I guess so," she replied, raising her eyebrows.

"I've never seen him drink before," I said.

"Me neither. He always told me he didn't like alcohol." I watched her swallow hard. "Whatever. Let's go outside."

We stepped toward the glass door and slid it open, walking outside. The cool breeze felt refreshing after only a few minutes inside the house. The patio was lit by two flood lights on both corners of the house. A ping-pong table was set up, taking up most of the concrete space. A large group of kids surrounded the table, shielding my view of what was going on in front of them. I watched as a tall, dark-haired guy lifted a ball and tossed it across the table and out of sight. A cheer went up around the table and the guy at the opposite end lifted a cup to his lips and drank it down. He belched loudly and everyone cheered again. Grass began where the patio ended. There were a few kids laying out across the lawn, gazing up at the stars. More kids stood at the edge of the yard, against a tall wood panel fence.

Mallory walked toward some folding chairs that were at the edge of the patio and sat down in one. She leaned forward with her elbows on her knees and looked out at everyone. Ryan sat down next to her, pulling his knees up close to his chest. I just stood, looking around at everything.

For everyone to be having so much fun, it all seemed kind of boring. Most of the people there were just laying around. While they were obviously drunk and high, they didn't seem to be doing much of anything.

And despite that, I felt strangely out of place. I'd entered some world that I wasn't a part of.

"This isn't what I thought it would be." Mallory said, watching another beer get downed at the ping pong table.

"What did you think it would be?" I asked.

She leaned back in her chair, crossing her hands over the stomach, "I don't know. I just thought this was something we had to do, you know? Like a rite of passage sort of thing. I think I'm just realizing now how little I know any of these people."

"I know how you feel," I replied. "Why do you think I only hang out with you guys? Most of the people at my school feel like strangers. I've been in the same class with them for twelve years and I feel like I get further away from them every year."

Mallory looked up at me, "It seems like it should be the other way around."

"Yeah, I guess. I mean, maybe all that matters is that we find our people, like I found you guys."

"Maybe you're right."

Looking out across the yard, I glanced at the faces of the people there. Most were West Haverty High kids. The people that were standing along the fence were mostly couples. Every few feet there was a guy and a girl either talking or making out against the fence. Only one person stood out. Standing in the middle of the fence was Milo Nash, cup in hand.

Milo and I had been friends in elementary school. We'd lived on the same street, so our moms frequently had us carpooling to school together. He would spend Saturday afternoons at my house while his parents went to run errands. I didn't remember a lot about those Saturdays, but I did remember Milo always being a really great friend. He was nice to me when everyone else in our class wasn't. His family had moved to Wisconsin before 6th grade, and I hadn't seen him sense.

He was leaning back against the wood, watching the kids laying out in the grass. I watched him take a sip and look up, his eyes landing on mine. I waved. He waved back and I could tell he remembered me from the surprise in his eyes.

"Hey, I'll be right back." I leaned down and kissed Ryan on the top of the head before walking across the yard, cutting through the starwatchers.

"Hi," I said when I reached him. "It's been a while. What are you doing here?"

His hair was messy, sticking up in several places, "My parents came back to visit some friends and dragged me along. I heard about the party from Mitch's brother. We were in Boy Scouts together."

"Oh, cool. So, how've you been?"

"Fine. You know, the usual. You?"

"I've been okay. Just ready to graduate."

"Yeah, me too."

He seemed different for some reason. He had always been quiet, but this wasn't the same. His jaw was tight, I could see the muscles moving beneath the skin. Every time he looked at someone around him, he would roll his eyes and take another sip from his cup. I could smell the alcohol on his breath from two feet away. He kept shifting his balance from one foot to the other.

I remembered him always being an awkward kid. Whenever we went to birthday parties for kids in our class, he would usually just eat his cake and make bad jokes. Now, he had lost that awkward presence. He seemed annoyed, almost bitter towards everything around him.

"Is everything okay?" I asked, looking around the yard and then back at him.

"I don't know, man." He took another sip, "I'm just fuckin' sick of this."

"Parties?"

"No, man, just all of it. The parties, high school, just fucking life."

"What do you mean?"

He finished the rest of his drink in one large sip and tossed the cup to the ground. "I just mean life, adulthood, everything. Seriously, what do we have to look forward to after graduation? Like, really? College debts and a shitty economy that isn't going to give us a job no matter what fucking degree we get. It's all just bullshit. We have to spend all this time in school because it'll help us get a good job and be successful, but the chances of that actually happening are really friggin' slim."

He wiped his hand across his mouth and sighed.

"It seems like things have been getting better lately," I said. "More jobs are getting created now."

He scoffed, "Man, even if that happens, what does it matter? Life'll still find a way to fuck you over in the end. Look at what happened to that teacher's son! He got hit by some asshole who was too stupid to take a cab home to his miserable life instead of driving. Now he's made someone else's life miserable and he just gets to keep living. See what I mean? The good ones get screwed over too. I mean there's so much shit in this world, man. So much fucking shit. Everybody just ignores it like it's gonna go away, but it's NOT. It's not gonna go away."

He let out another sigh and leaned his head back against the fence.

We hadn't spoken since he moved so I had no way of knowing what was going on in his life, but I never would have imagined him getting like this. As kids, he'd always been so hopeful, positive. Whenever I would get hurt or sad, he would always have something to tell me that would make me not feel as bad. I could still see him sitting next to me on the sidewalk after I'd fallen off my bike for the tenth time and him telling me that I would get it eventually, that it took him a long time too.

Now, hearing him talk, it was like being with a stranger. He was so bitter, so angry. I had never been around anyone who was that pissed at life before.

I swallowed, unsure of what to say.

"I'm sorry, man," he said, looking at me again and standing up away from the fence. He closed his eyes and rubbed a hand across his face. "I've just had a bad night. It was nice seeing you though." He stepped forward and walked back to the house.

I stood there for a moment, feeling blindsided by the change in him. What had happened to him? Would he be different if we hadn't lost touch? If he hadn't moved and we had stayed friends maybe I could have helped him somehow. I wasn't sure what I could have done, but maybe it would have kept him from getting like this, getting so angry.

A hand took mine and I turned to see Ryan standing just behind me. "Hey," he said. "You okay?"

"I think so." I replied, though I didn't believe myself.

He pulled me forward to an empty spot in the yard and we laid down too, looking up at the stars. I held his hand between us as we lay there.

I thought about everything Milo had said. What if he was right? So much was going wrong in the lives of the people around me. Mrs. Stroud losing her son, Kevin and Jeremy's money problems, Mallory already making choices that didn't coincide with what she wanted for her life. My mom. Nothing was going right, and everything seemed to be going wrong. Everyone around me was unhappy in some way. They didn't deserve any of the pain they were feeling. What if Milo was right? A nervous dread pooled in my stomach.

I didn't know how long we'd been laying there before Mallory found us. She stood over us with her hands on her hips. We both sat up.

"Have you seen Kevin? I don't know where he is."

I stood up, Ryan doing the same next to me, "No, I haven't. Have you looked inside?"

"Yeah, I can't find him anywhere and it's kind of worrying me." She bit her lip and looked around the yard. "Let's go."

We walked across the yard and back into the house. People were still standing around talking, only now more bottles were empty on the island. I scanned the room looking for Kevin. He didn't seem to be among the people in the kitchen, so we moved into the living room. Not there either. We checked all the rooms down the hall, but they were filled with more people smoking or passed out. Making our way back to the living room, we stepped across people on the floor and walked out into the front yard.

There he was.

Kevin was sitting out in the grass, an empty bottle next to him. We walked over to him and Mallory picked up the bottle.

"Kevin, what are you doing?" she asked, the bottle hanging from her hand at her side.

Kevin leaned back to look at her with eyes that were clouded by alcohol. His eye lids drooped low, his jaw hanging loose. Sweat matted his black curls to his forehead.

"I-I'm, Imhavingfuuuun." he replied, words slurring together. He reached for the bottle in Mallory's hand, but she held it away. His eyes narrowed as he looked at it. "Guess I need s'more."

Legs wobbling, he got to his feet and tried to move towards the house. Mallory and I stepped forward to block his path.

"I think we should go, Kevin" I said, putting my hand on his shoulder.

He shoved it off, "No, I'm goonnna stay."

"Kevin." Mallory sighed and tossed the bottle behind her, "We're leaving. Come on."

He rolled his eyes. "Nooo."

"Kevin. Now."

"Ugggh," he grunted. "Fine."

Turning, he wobbled across the lawn and began walking down the sidewalk. We followed, Ryan taking my hand as we walked. When we got to the car, Kevin stepped around to the driver's side.

"Whoa, Kevin, no!" Mallory ran around and stopped him, moving herself between him and the door. "Give me your keys." Her voice stern and forceful.

"No, it's myyy car. Ima gonna drive my car." He tried to reach past her to open the door, but she wouldn't budge. "Mallory! Move!" he yelled.

She grabbed his arm and pushed him back. Ryan and I stepped off the curb and into the street where Kevin was turning around with his hands on his head.

"Kevin, I think you should let Mallory drive. Come on, don't be stupid." I said.

"I'm not stupid!" he yelled, turning to me and holding his arms out at his sides, his eyes getting big. "I'm not stupid."

"Okay," I replied. "I'm sorry, just please give Mallory your keys. You're not in the right mind to drive, Kevin. Please."

He reached in his pocket and pulled out his keys, throwing them on the ground between him and Mallory, "Here! Take'em! I'm gonna stay." He moved past us and back up onto the sidewalk. Turning back toward the house, he started walking.

We ran past and stopped in front of him, blocking his path.

"Kevin, it's time to go. Come on. We're leaving." I said, putting a hand on his arm and pointing back to the car.

"I SAID I'M STAYING!" he yelled at us. He stepped back, hands balling into fists at his sides and his face turning red. He looked furious.

"And we said that we're leaving." Mallory said, calm, but firm. "This isn't you, Kevin. You're more responsible than this."

His hands came up and into his hair, his nails digging into his scalp. He spoke through gritted teeth, "Maybe I'm tired of being responsible."

"Kevin- "

"No! I'm tired of it. Why'm I always the one who has to fix things?! Why'm I always the one who has to take caaare of everyone?! I'm so tired of taking care of EVERYthing! I'm tired of studying and working all the time! I feel like I can't *breathe* sometimes! It never endsss! I just want one day where I'm not thinking about everyone else and if theeey're okay. I just want one day for meee!" Tears filled his eyes and slid down his cheeks. His hands stayed in his hair and his body began to shake violently with sobs. "I'm so TIRED. I'm so tired."

My breath caught in my throat as he fell to his knees in the middle of the sidewalk, leaning his head down against the pavement. His shoulders shook as he continued to cry and cry, into the sidewalk.

"I'm so tired. I'm tired. I'm tired." He sobbed.

The dread pooled deeper in my stomach as I watched him cry. Kevin was the one who never broke.

I turned to Mallory, hoping she would know what to say to him, what to do for him. Her mouth hung open, tears on her own cheeks.

"Kevin . . ." Nothing more came out.

I watched him crying there on the sidewalk and felt sick. This was what Milo was talking about, the way life chewed you up and spit you out. Even the best ones didn't get off easy.

I stepped forward and fell to my knees in front of him. Reaching forward, I grasped each of his sweaty hands in my own and held them tightly.

Out of the corner of my eye, I saw Ryan move. He sat down next to Kevin on the ground and reached one hand across Kevin's back, laying the side of his head down against the top of Kevin's shoulder.

After a moment, Mallory knelt beside us and gently placed a hand on Kevin's shoulder. Turning him onto his side, his head fell into her lap and she brought a hand up to his forehead. Like that night in my bedroom, she brushed his sweaty curls away from his eyes. This time, she didn't care if we saw.

Kevin's face was red, tears flowing from his eyes and around his nose to stain Mallory's denim covered legs. He didn't look at any of us, just sobbed quietly into her lap.

My chest tightened as we knelt on the sidewalk. I felt like I wanted to cry, but the tears wouldn't come. An ache began in my chest and it wouldn't release. Kevin was so unhappy and I couldn't see an end for it. What if he didn't get the scholarship? What would he do, staying here, working his life away? Everything was so hard for him and he was right, he deserved some kind of relief. He deserved some rest. And it wasn't there.

Kevin finally stopped shaking and moved to sit up. His face was red, his eyes puffy and lips loose. He lifted a hand and wiped at his eyes. He leaned forward, wrapping his arms around my neck. I slid my arms around his back and just held him. His warm breath was against my neck, his sniffles in my ears. Maybe there wasn't anything we could say to make him feel better. Maybe all we could do was be there, like he was always there for us.

Eventually, he let go of me and sat back on his heels. "Let'ss go home," he said, his voice deep and heavy with tears.

We helped him up and stepped over to the car. Mallory picked up the keys off the pavement and we all got in, Kevin in the passenger seat. Ryan slid in close to me in the back seat, leaning his head on my shoulder. I looked out the window as we pulled away to see if anybody had been watching us. There were two guys standing on the sidewalk across the street just staring at us. I wondered if they had heard what Kevin said, if they understood his pain.

Mallory drove to my house first, dropping me off at the end of the driveway. I kissed Ryan goodnight and he looked at me, holding my hand for a moment longer before letting me get out of the car. As I walked up the driveway, I turned to see them drive away. He watched me out the window with a curious face. A few seconds later, as I reached the door, I got a text:

RYAN: *Are you okay?*

ME: *I just don't feel good.*

I put my phone in my pocket and unlocked the door. The house was dark and quiet when I stepped inside. I walked through the kitchen and into the living room. It had been a while since it had been this quiet. I didn't like it. It felt cold and uncomfortable. The sickness in my stomach churned.

Walking up the stairs, I stopped outside my mom's room. On the other side of the door, I could hear her soft snores. She wasn't lying awake crying like she had for weeks on end. She was actually sleeping. I felt like I should be happy about it, but I couldn't. The ache in my chest felt tight and strong and I couldn't feel anything else. I went in my room and sat down on my bed, trying to take deep breaths.

Breathe in. Breathe out. Breathe In. Breathe Out.

Nothing. No relief. The sickness stayed.

I looked around my room. My eyes fell on the picture frame on my desk. I couldn't see the picture in the darkness, but I knew what it looked like. I could see my parents and me in Chicago, somewhere on Michigan Avenue, smiles on our faces. We looked happy. To the outside observer we would seem happy. It was wrong. It was all wrong. No one was happy.

I turned and looked at my closet. Had Brooke been happy? How could she have been? It seemed like she was having just as many problems as I was, so how could she be happy if I wasn't?

My breathing quickened, the sickness in my stomach growing, the ache spreading throughout my chest. I got up and went out into the hall and down the stairs. I looked around our living room, the place of so many nights together, movies and popcorn, the place of so many of my parents' fights. The kitchen was the same, more sad memories than good. What room in the house wasn't like that?

My heart beat faster. I had to get out. I had to leave this place, this house. I ran out the door, yanking it shut behind me before running down the driveway and down the sidewalk. I ran and ran and ran, my heart beating faster and faster in my chest. I turned down streets, not paying attention to where I was going, just needing to keep running. My feet slammed into the pavement, my shins starting to ache. I kept running, the world going quiet around me. The only sound I could hear was the sound of my heart beating in my chest, in my entire body. It thumped loudly in my ears and whacked against my rib cage. My breath caught in my throat.

I finally had to stop running out of fear that I would stop breathing completely. Looking up, I was in a playground surrounded by houses. There was a swing set, a slide, and a merry-go-round. I had been here before when I was little. The swing set was more rusted now. I walked forward, grabbing ahold of one of the metal bars supporting the swing set. Leaning my forehead against it, I felt the cold metal press into my skin. My breathing wasn't slowing down. Stopping had done nothing. I was scared. Tears welled in my eyes, clouding my vision. I heard a whimper from somewhere and realized it was my own voice. I gripped the metal bar tightly, praying that everything would stop. *God, help me, please, help me. I'm scared.* My heart continued thumping and I clutched a hand to my chest. What would happen if I died here? Who would find me? What would they say? What would happen to my mom?

I pulled my phone out of my pocket, my hands shaking as I pressed on Ryan's number. The phone felt heavy in my hand as I held it to my ear.

Ring. My chest clenched tighter.

Ring. My breathing felt short and fast.

Click. "Peter?"

"Ryan."

A breath filled my lungs at the sound of his voice, a small relief. I tried to think of what to say, not sure how to put what I was feeling into words.

"I...I can't."

"What's wrong, Peter?"

I tried to take a deep breath, "I-I don't know . . . I just . . ."

How could I put it into words when I couldn't even catch my breath? When everything around me wouldn't stop spinning?

"Where are you? Are you at home?"

"No, I'm-I'm at that park on Avondale Road."

"Okay, stay there. I'm coming."

There was a click, and I slipped the phone back into my pocket. A soft breeze cooled the sweat on my neck. The hinges of the swings creaked as they swayed back and forth. I looked around me. There were houses around the playground and I wondered who was sleeping behind the dark windows. Were they okay? Were they hurting too?

I was still sitting by the swing when Ryan rode up on his bicycle. He dropped his bike in the grass by the street and came running over to me. His arms went around me and my head fell to his shoulder.

In the ten minutes it had taken him to get there, my breathing had slowed down. The thumping in my chest began to subside. Now that he was here, I finally started to feel my head clear.

Pulling away, I looked at him. His eyes glowed in the moonlight. The breeze ruffled his hair.

"I'm sorry I called you," I said, leaning my head back against the metal bar of the swing set. "I just didn't know what to do."

He took my hand, rubbing his thumb over my knuckles. "You don't have anything to be sorry for. What happened?"

I stared at the ground, watching the dirt shift slightly every time a breeze came through. My head hurt. It felt full of so many different things and I couldn't sort through it all to get to something to tell Ryan. I could still see Kevin crouched down in the middle of the sidewalk, could see my mom crying at the kitchen table, Mrs. Stroud's face as she wailed over her dead son's body. I could see all of them so clearly, feel their pain like it was mine. It was just all too much, and I didn't know what to do.

"I just feel like a couple weeks from now we're all going to be shoved out into the world and the only thing I can think about is how terrified I am." I sighed.

"What are you afraid of?" Ryan asked, still running his thumb across my hand.

"I . . ." I began and then stopped. I couldn't do that. I couldn't unload on Ryan, not after everything he'd been through. He'd been so depressed that he'd tried to take his own life. There was no way I was going to put my pain onto him. "I can't do this. I'm not going to give you my troubles, Ryan."

"Peter, it's fine."

"No. No, it's not. *I'm* supposed to be the one helping *you*, saving you. Not the other way around."

"But you do," his thumb stopped moving and he took my whole hand in his. His eyes met mine, "You save me every day."

I opened my mouth to speak, but nothing came out. What could I say to that? I had never really thought about the affect our relationship had on him. Obviously, I'd always tried to make him feel comfortable and safe with me. I knew that was working, but maybe it had gone deeper than that. Maybe somewhere between comfortable and safe he'd begun to heal. He was certainly doing better than when I'd met him. Maybe by loving him I was helping lessen his pain, helping him feel more secure in his own skin. What if, maybe, I had been helping him all along?

"Peter," Ryan leaned in, pressing his forehead to mine. "Please let me help you."

I closed my eyes, inhaling his warm breath into mine. "It just seems like everything is going wrong and it's just going to keep going wrong."

"You mean with your parents?"

"No . . . yes . . . I don't know," I leaned forward, my face resting in my palms. My head felt heavy. "She's just so unhappy still." Her crying face flashed in my mind, "She's been so upset for so long and there's nothing I can do about it."

"Maybe she just has to grieve for a while. I don't think there's a time limit on things like this. I mean, it's taken me years to feel better about what happened to me." He squeezed my hand.

"I just feel so helpless. It's like all I can do is sit around and watch her hurt." The breeze blew across my face and I realized I had tears on my cheeks again.

Ryan didn't say anything, just sat there watching me.

"I feel so angry lately. Why did he do this? Why did my father hurt us like this?"

"Maybe he didn't have any other choice." he said.

I stood up, walking away a few steps to look at him. I ran my fingers through my sweaty hair, "What do you mean? He could have stayed. He had a choice, and he chose to hurt us." I knew Ryan was trying to help, but I just couldn't understand how my father wouldn't have a choice. This was all his fault.

Ryan looked up at me, his hands coming together in his lap, eyes soft as always. "But you said they weren't happy together?"

"So? They're certainly not happy *now*." I turned and looked around at the dark trees and shadowed fences. The thumping in my chest was coming back.

"But maybe now they can try to be." His voice was quiet behind me, "My therapist keeps telling me that part of being happy is choosing it. She says I have to choose to be happy for it to actually happen. Maybe that's what your father did. Maybe this was the only choice that led to some kind happiness."

I turned back to him, sitting there on the ground. He watched me, like he was waiting for me to do something. I took a deep breath and walked back over to him, sitting down.

"I'm sorry I'm so frustrated."

"Stop apologizing," he said, pressing his cheek into my shoulder and inhaling through his nose.

Leaning my head back, I looked up at the stars. There were a few clouds floating across the sky. I counted the stars I could see, thinking of a different person in my life with each one. Mom. Kevin. Mallory. Ryan. Mrs. Stroud.

"I hate what happened to Mrs. Stroud's son. I hate it."

Out of the corner of my eye, I saw Ryan follow my gaze up. "Me too."

"I hate that people die before they're supposed to. I hate funerals. I hate that life is so fucking hard." Tears filled my eyes again, "I hate that Kevin and Jeremy are having so much trouble. Why do they have to struggle so much? Why doesn't Kevin get the chance to enjoy being young like the rest of us? It's not fair. He works so hard and it just doesn't make a difference. He's just had so much bad stuff happen to him. Is that really what life is going to be like?"

"I don't know. I used to think I'd never get to a point in my life where I didn't feel bad." Ryan leaned his head back down on my shoulder and took my hand in his.

"What do you think now?" I said, quietly.

He was silent for a minute before responding, "Now I think that, maybe, it'll be okay. I have you and I have Kevin and I have Mallory. Maybe I can handle the bad times because of that."

I thought about the moments that I'd felt happiest over the past few months. They had been there for all of them. Kevin and Mallory running through the park, Ryan laughing at the carnival. Thinking about them made the thumping in my chest get a little better.

"How am I supposed to help the people around me feel like that?"

"I don't know. Maybe you already do without realizing it. You do it for me." He lifted his head and looked at me.

I pressed my lips to his gently and held them there for a moment, feeling his face relax against mine.I pulled away and looked back up at the sky. The clouds had moved past and I could see all the stars now. Inhaling, the smells of the night filled my nose. I exhaled. My chest still felt tight and my head hurt, but it was a little better now. I felt like I could breathe a little easier for the moment. Getting up, I held my hand out to Ryan to help him stand.

"Let's go."

We walked back to my house in the light of the streetlamps. Neither of us said a word, just letting the soft sounds of his bike tires against the pavement fill the silence. It seemed so much more peaceful now. When I had been running, it had felt like there was chaos all around me, but now it was quiet. When we got to my door, Ryan came inside with me. The house was still silent. He sent his mom a text that we were all going to have an all-nighter at my house, so he wouldn't be home till morning. We went up to my room and got into my bed, his chest pressing into my back and an arm going around me. I listened to the soft sounds of my mom snoring across the hall, felt the warmth of Ryan's breath against my neck. Within minutes we were both asleep.

32

My father texted me the next morning asking if we could meet. I didn't want to, but I was worried he would try to come to the house if I said no. He said I could come by his apartment, or we could meet somewhere. I told him I would come to him. I knew what he was going to talk to me about and that wasn't a conversation I wanted to have in public.

His apartment complex consisted of three brick buildings on Stanford Avenue. It was a nice little area, lots of flowers everywhere and a pool.

I walked to the farthest building and knocked on the door of 1-C. My stomach felt like it was twisting up inside of me. I didn't want to talk, didn't want to go through this with him, but I couldn't just run away. That wouldn't make anything better.

He answered the door in a t-shirt and jeans, his black hair wet like he'd just gotten out of the shower. He looked as nervous as I did, his mouth opening and closing a couple times before he got any words out.

"Hey, come on in."

His apartment was surprisingly empty. The only items in the one room were a bed, a dresser, and a table. There was a small kitchenette off to the left side of the room. A box of cereal and a bowl of apples sat atop the small counter. There was a doorway in the back-left corner across from the kitchen that I assumed was the bathroom. His bed was made up with off-white sheets that I knew he'd packed with him when he'd moved out. There was no nightstand, just an upside-down cardboard box with a clock on it sitting next to the bed.

It was weird to see him living like this. It wasn't bad. He still had everything he needed. It was just strange to go from seeing him in our house with all its random crap sitting around to this one room with a bed.

"We can sit at the table if you want." He stepped over and pulled out a chair. "Do you want something to drink? I have water or Diet Coke." He moved around the room quickly, pulling two glasses from one of the cabinets above the sink.

"Water's fine." I sat down at the table and watched him fill the glasses with tap water before coming to sit down across from me.

We sipped the water and sat quietly for a minute. I wasn't sure if I was supposed to say something. I felt like I shouldn't have to since he was the one who wanted to meet. It was his talk.

Finally he spoke, "Um, so I wanted to talk to you after our last dinner together. Things didn't go exactly how I'd planned them."

"How had you planned them to go?" I said, making sure to keep my voice calm.

"I just . . . I don't know. I don't know how to do this, Peter. I'm supposed to, right? I'm the dad. This shouldn't be this hard."

He didn't look at me, just stared at the glass in his hands. Somewhere inside me, I felt pity for him. He seemed so nervous, like he was under pressure. As mad as I was, I thought about what Ryan had said about choosing happiness. Maybe it wasn't an easy decision to make.

"This isn't easy for me either."

He looked up at me and for the first time in a long time, our eyes met. His seemed so sad and weak as he stared at me.

"I'm your father. I'm supposed to make it easier for you. You shouldn't have to feel pressure like this. I've failed you, Peter. I thought I could make things better for you and your mother if we separated, but I've just pushed you away. I thought everyone would be better, happier. I thought it would help me get closer to you."

I looked at my father, watched his eyes fill up with tears, and felt like I was finally seeing him for the first time. Maybe he wasn't who I thought he was. Maybe Ryan was right, and he'd made a choice for happiness and maybe it wasn't what he'd expected it to be. I didn't know how to fix our situation, but he didn't either. And that was okay. I was starting to realize that being an adult didn't mean you had all the answers. You couldn't always fix everything. But maybe admitting when you're lost, like my father was doing now, was the next best thing you could do.

"Maybe we can keep trying, like keep having dinner. I would be okay with that."

My father looked up at me.

"Are you sure? I don't want you to be miserable with me."

I nodded, "Yeah, I'm sure. And we don't have to be miserable. We can try harder. Together, I mean."

His eyes perked up slightly. "I'd like that. I'd like that a lot."

We sat there for a little while longer, talking about school and his job. It wasn't perfect, but we were working at it and maybe that was the only thing we could do.

33

It was one of those perfect mornings. We were all in the kitchen. An early sun was shining through the window, washing the walls in an orange glow. The smell of pancakes and cooking spray danced in the air. Soft plops of flipped batter were back drop to our whispers and laughter.

Kevin, Mallory, Ryan, and I sat at the counter coloring in superhero comic books we'd purchased at Walgreens. Kevin was arguing with Mallory about her choice to change Spiderman's colors to green and purple to which she responded by laughing maniacally. Ryan and I were deep into a discussion about the proper shading of a tree in a Wonder Woman picture. Our hair was a mess and our clothes were wrinkled from falling asleep in the living room the night before.

Mom was at the stove making the pancakes with Grandma. She had a smile on her face as she laughed at our jokes. Her shoulders were relaxed in her pink robe. It was nice seeing her so at ease. The stove light lit up her face as she turned to set plates full of crisp bacon and slightly burned pancakes in front of each of us.

She'd been getting up every day since her talk with Grandma, making her bed and preparing her lunch. She wasn't better yet. Her eyes would still be red some mornings from crying, but she was taking steps to get to a happier place. She and Grandma had spent the past weekend at a spa. It seemed to help.

Kevin reached for the maple syrup, dumping a third of it on his plate in thick globs. Mallory swiped her hand across the back of his head, yelling at him for taking so much. His response was to turn the bottle upside down and dump the second third onto her plate. She continued yelling. It was all ridiculous and hilarious.

There were a lot of things in my life that weren't exactly how I wanted them to be, but in that moment I didn't care. I was happy, I was with people I cared about, and that was enough.

It was Saturday night. We'd all spent the evening on my couch watching one of the Spiderman movies. Kevin and Mallory had gone home so it was just Ryan and me. He was asleep, his head laying on a pillow at the end of the couch and his legs pulled up against him as tight as possible. His sock clad toes brushed against the outside of my thigh. He'd fallen asleep toward the end of the movie, his hand holding mine against his hip. At some point in his sleep he'd let go, his hand releasing mine and falling to rest against his stomach. Every few minutes, he would shift slightly, pulling his arms and legs tighter against himself. A shiver would pass through his body.

I reached down to the opposite end of the couch and picked up the blanket that Mallory had been using. Spreading it wide, I draped it across his body. I pressed the edges in tight against his sides and around his arms and legs. The only part I left free was the space where his toes pressed against my thigh. Though so small, there was something about it that I liked. Maybe it was how when I closed my eyes I could still feel him, that small touch bringing sense to my world. I watched him sleep, the soft breathing fluttering the loose strands at the edge of the blanket by his neck.

I loved him. It seemed so small, those words, but it didn't feel small. My love for him felt big and all encompassing. My love for him felt like everything. It weighed down my heart and yet it felt like it was bouncing out of my chest. My love for him made me ache and smile and laugh and cry. My love for him was all of me.

It was different than I thought it would be. It had always seemed nice, the idea of being in love. I watched other people go around, hand in hand, and I thought about what it would feel like to have another person be in my life in that way. In my mind, it never felt this . . . much. I had never pictured it feeling like there was some piece locking into place, filling a space that had never seemed empty before then.

I thought about my mom and all the pain she was feeling. For the longest time I had thought it was because of my father, because of how much he had hurt her. And it was, it was that, but even more than that it was a loss of this. She was hurting because she had lost love. Sitting there on the couch, watching that beautiful boy sleep, I understood it. Being able to live with everything I was feeling at that moment for over twenty years of marriage seemed like a blessing. The thought of losing it, that feeling that felt so whole and complete, was impossible. It was too painful to think about. After months and months watching her hurt, I felt like I finally got it, I finally understood. I still ached for her, but now I felt peace of mind. Her pain didn't seem so foreign to me and in some ways that made it easier.

I looked over at Ryan sleeping so gently beside me. I couldn't imagine losing him, I couldn't imagine losing this boy that made me feel this way. He made me feel alive, made me feel real.

Ryan's eyes fluttered open, and he turned his head slightly to look at me.

"I love you," I whispered into the quiet and it was true. I love you, Ryan. I love this boy. I love him. I love him, I love him, I love him.

"I love you too," he whispered back to me, and I felt nothing else but him.

34

The night before graduation, Mallory picked me up from my house and we went and got burgers at McDonalds. Kevin and Ryan were both busy, so it was just the two of us. We rode through the drive-thru and then sat in the parking lot beneath the sign and ate. The yellow light from above us shone down through the windshield, illuminating the dashboard. A slow rock song played on the radio. Mallory wiped her mouth with a napkin and pulled the tie out of her hair, letting it flow down around her shoulders.

"I'm going to USC." She said, taking another bite of her burger. "I committed a few months ago. I just didn't say anything to you guys about it because I knew you wouldn't be happy."

I looked over at her. She hadn't said anything about college since she'd announced what schools she'd gotten into.

"It's the best physical therapy program out of the options I have, and California could be nice, so . . ." She didn't look at me. I watched as her eyes moved up the windshield to the big arch above our heads. The yellow and red light glowed in her eyes. "And I know what you're going to say about the fact that I'm not going for photography, so please don't. I can still take photographs and go to school for PT. LA's a big city. There will be plenty of opportunities for me to keep using my camera. I'm not giving it up. I'm just . . ." Her eyes fell to the steering wheel in front of her. "I'm just letting it come second. And that's okay. Second isn't gone."

Mallory reached down and picked up a fry, tossing it into her mouth. She seemed calm and confident, just like she always did. I wondered if she was telling me because I was the only one who was free that night or if it was because she knew I wouldn't argue with her about it like Kevin or Ryan might. And I wasn't going to argue. She had made up her mind and, knowing Mallory, that meant the discussion was finished. She seemed content though. In the past few months, whenever the subject had come up, she had quickly gotten frustrated. Now she was relaxed and seemingly sure of herself. And, for once, I felt like she was okay. Like she said, second wasn't gone. She wasn't giving up what she loved and that was what mattered.

"Okay," I said, watching as she looked over at me briefly and smiled.

"I'll be happy." she said, her eyes locked with mine. "I promise I will."

And that was what was important.

35

I woke up early on the morning of my graduation ceremony. I hadn't planned on it, but I just woke up and couldn't go back to sleep for the rest of the hour before my alarm was set to go off. Laying there under the covers, gazing out my window, I thought about what was going to happen within the next few hours. Everyone had told me through the years that graduating high school was going to be one of the biggest days of my life. Strangely, the more I thought about it, it didn't feel that big. I didn't feel like I was about to "end an era" or "close a chapter" or any of the other things people were always saying about this day. It just felt like a day where I had to go to this ceremony and walk across a stage in front of a large group of people. Frankly, that was more nerve-wracking than the thought of graduating. I hated being the center of attention or getting up in front of people. It made my palms sweat and my heart race. It was an incredibly awkward situation and I was not looking forward to having to do it that morning.

I turned over and my mind drifted to elementary school and middle school and how I'd changed over the years. In elementary school, I had been somewhat shy. Milo was my best friend and I was happy. We had the traditional sleepovers and birthday parties. Once middle school came and Milo moved, I became kind of a loner, not really having any real friends for a while. I stuck more to myself and spent my evenings writing in my room alone. That continued into high school. Once high school began and we all had more freedom, I distanced myself from everyone even more. When everyone around me was acting so different from me and doing things that I just wasn't into, I didn't feel the need to engage with anyone. And then I finally met Kevin, Mallory, and Ryan. It didn't occur to me until I met them how much I *needed* people like them in my life, real friends. For so long I had thought I was fine being on my own, that, unlike everyone else, I didn't need other people. But I did and I didn't even see it. Despite everything that had been going on over the past several months, I was happier than I had ever been. I was happier because of them, because of how I felt when I was with them. I felt like I was a part of something, like we belonged to each other in such a special way.

And Ryan. That amazing boy who was all mine. He was the sweetest part of it all. I felt more love for him than I thought I could feel for any-one. He was truly the most amazing person I had ever met, and I was so thankful that I got to love him and help heal his pain and just be *his*.

The night before, I picked up my notebook to do some writing. When I opened it to the back to start on the next blank page, I had found something written in the top margin:

If I could, I would put all your pain onto me so you could feel free again.

I recognized Ryan's handwriting and my eyes filled with tears when I read it. He had hurt so much in his life, hurt more than anyone should have to at our age. The thought of him wanting to take my own pain onto himself just so I could be happy broke my heart. Ryan wasn't somebody who said things he didn't mean. His words were so few and so rare that he only said what he meant. This sweet, beautiful boy who would take on more pain for my happiness simply took my breath away. His heart was so much bigger than himself and I got to hold a place in it. I thanked God that I got to have this boy in my life.

My mother eventually came and knocked on my door. When she opened it, she peeked her head around the door at me, still laying in the bed. A smile lit up her face.

"What are you doing? Today's the big day! You have to get up!" There was a lightness in her voice that I hadn't heard in so long and I smiled as it filled my heart with love for my mom.

"I don't need to get up for another thirty minutes." I said, leaning up on my elbows.

She opened the door further and I could see that she was already in a bright blue dress with white flowers around the neck. Pearl earrings that my father had given her were in her ears. "If you want the breakfast I'm making you, you better get out of that bed now and get your butt ready."

I smiled and flipped the covers back, hopping out of the bed and walking over to my closet door. Pulling out khaki's, a white button down, and the tie that I planned to wear, I laid them across the end of the bed. When I turned back to my mom, there were tears on her cheeks. Unlike the past few months, these looked like happy tears.

"Oh," she said, walking over to me and looking down at my clothes. "I've been thinking about this day since you were little. I never thought it would get here so quickly. It feels like I've spent so much time being your mother that I don't know what I'll do now that you're going off to college. I don't know what the next chapter is for me."

I turned to her, "You're still my mom. That doesn't change."

"I know, but you won't need me anymore."

"I'll always need you, Mom." I reached out and hugged her, wrapping my arms tightly around her. She hugged me back before stepping away.

She wiped the tears from her eyes and said, "Maybe I'll start volunteering somewhere when I'm not working. The women's shelter is always looking for people, maybe I could help out there."

She smiled and for the first time in a long time, it seemed like my mom was on solid ground. It seemed like maybe she would be okay after all, that I could go away in the fall and not have to worry about whether or not she was falling apart. I could go on with my life and so could she. We could be okay together.

The school was already crowded by the time we pulled into the parking lot. My mom and grandma dropped me off at the door before going to find a parking space. I pushed my way through the crowd of parents and grandparents until I got to the chemistry classroom where we were supposed to all meet. Everyone was already in the process of getting on their caps and gowns. The room was filled with people in navy blue, adjusting and zipping themselves in. I had known most of these people for years and even though I hadn't been close to a lot of them, it felt strange that this was the last time we would all be in the same place.

Once the time came, we all got in line and began walking to the gym. As the music started playing and we began processing in from the back, I looked around for Kevin, Mallory, and Ryan. I could see the top of their heads through the crowd, standing next to my parents and grandma. They weren't graduating until the following Saturday due to an agreement between the two high schools to avoid overlapping ceremonies. They all smiled at me as I approached their row.

My mother and father stood next to each other. My father was wearing the same blue suit he'd been wearing to events all my life. His face was shaved clean and his hair was combed. He looked nice and I wondered if it was partially due to his new girlfriend. Maybe she was like my mom and reminded him to shave before nice events. Maybe she was nothing like my mom and he had just learned how to clean up well from all their years together. I wondered if his new girlfriend made him happy, happy like he'd been when I was little. When I looked at him now, I didn't feel the anger that I'd been feeling for months and months now. He wasn't trying to hurt us. He just wanted to be happy again. I passed by him and my mom and my friends and gave them all a little wave. They all waved back, and I thought to myself that maybe I could be happy for my father and his new girlfriend. If she was able to make him happy, happy in a way that he couldn't find with my mom anymore, than maybe that was okay. Maybe we all just needed to find someplace happier.

We took our seats in the front few rows. The speeches and awards began. Erin Dempsey was valedictorian and she stood up and made what was a really nice speech about going out into the world and being who we were meant to be.

They began calling our names to come up on the stage. I watched as people I'd known since childhood got up, walked across the stage, and took their diploma, stopping to pose for parental photos of them holding their diploma case. It seemed kind of odd, the ritual of it, the sameness of it all. I looked at their smiling faces and wondered what they were thinking as they stood there. Were they thinking of all the years we'd been together? All the classes we all sat through?

"Peter Hansen."

I swallowed hard and began walking up the steps to the stage. My heart beat faster as I reached the top and began to walk across to Principal Hughes, his arm extended to me, ready to be shaken. I focused on him and not the people watching me and clapping. I shook his hand and took my diploma, stepping past him to stand where all my other classmates had. I stopped and looked out at the crowd and instead of feeling nervous, I felt a smile spread across my face. There they were, my friends. Kevin, Mallory, and Ryan were standing up next to my parents. Kevin was holding up a big poster board with "You didn't fail!" written in big letters across it. Mallory's face was covered with her camera as she took pictures of me, stopping at one point to gesture to me to hold my diploma higher. My eyes fell on Ryan. He didn't have a poster or a camera, he just had his sweet smile and that was enough. My family were all taking photos, my mom and grandma with their digital cameras and my father with his phone. I stood there for a moment longer looking out at all of them, my people, before going down the steps and into whatever was next.

After the ceremony, everyone went outside to take pictures. As I walked through the crowd searching for my parents, I found Mrs. Stroud. She was speaking to another student, shaking his hand, and telling him to work hard in college. When she said goodbye to him, she turned to me. Her eyes looked tired despite her make-up and the smile she gave me only went so far up her cheeks.

"Hey, I didn't expect to see you here."

"I wanted to see everyone. I've watched you all over the past four years and I wasn't going to miss seeing you walk across that stage." She replied, holding out her arms and giving me a warm hug.

When she stepped back, she looked me in the eyes. "Now, tell me you've still been writing."

I nodded, "I have, and I've actually found my ending."

She looked at me curiously, "Oh, really? And what did you come to?"

"Amber leaves, but I think Connor'll eventually be okay with it. It's not the happiest ending, but it feels like the most honest."

"I knew you would find it. You just had to discover it on your own." She smiled at me, and for a moment I thought I could see the old Mrs. Stroud, the one who was happy and sarcastic and tough. That person was still there, just dimmer. It made me feel like maybe she would be okay, too, eventually. I didn't expect her to ever get past her son's death, not really, but maybe she could get someplace better than where she was now. "Well, I better go say goodbye to some of the others. It was really nice seeing you, Peter. I'm so proud of you. If you'd like, I'd love to read your new pages."

"Thanks. I'm glad I got to see you, too. And I'd really like that. I hope you're doing better."

She smiled, "One day at a time."

I watched as she walked away to talk to other students and knew that she was right. Better was coming. One day at a time.

I found my family near the flagpole in the front of the school yard. My mom gave me a long hug and cried a little bit into my shoulder before letting go.

"I'm so happy to have you as my son," she said, stepping back.

My grandma kissed my forehead, squeezing my shoulders gently.

My father gave a shorter hug, patting me on the back and holding his hand on my shoulder long enough to say, "I'm proud of you, son."

"Thanks," I said, smiling at him.

My mom didn't stand directly next to my father. She lingered a couple feet away from him, but other than that she was surprisingly fine around him. They had seen each other only at meetings with the lawyers, this being the first time outside of that. I was proud of my mom for being so comfortable around him. I took a picture with each of them and then one with us all together. It was okay. It all felt okay.

Kevin, Mallory, and Ryan had found us by then.

"Oh my gosh," Mallory said, throwing her arms around me. "This one had to pee like a pregnant woman." She pointed at Kevin as she let go of me.

"Hey, it was a long ceremony. That principal of yours likes to talk." Kevin replied, holding up his hands in defense.

Ryan stepped over to my side and wrapped his arms around me. I put an arm around his shoulder and kissed the side of his head.

"All right, you guys all stand together so I can get a picture!" My mother called out.

Kevin and Mallory came around to my other side, Mallory slipping her arm through mine and leaning her head against my shoulder. Kevin put his arm across her back and we all smiled as my mother took photo after photo after photo. The people that I loved were at my side, all smiling and happy.

When I got back home, I went up to my room. Pulling a sharpie out of my desk drawer, I went and sat down in the bottom of my closet. I gazed over Brooke's messages and found an empty spot in the center. Next to all her words, I left one of my own.

Let's be okay

"I don't feel any different."

Kevin was sitting in the passenger seat of Mallory's car. We were at Sonic, windows rolled down and doors open to let the summer breeze blow through. Ryan and I sat in the back, his body stretched out across the seat, head in my lap. My hand holding his over his chest.

It was Sunday afternoon, their graduation ceremony was the day before. It had been a nice ceremony, similar to mine. I had cheered and taken pictures next to Jeremy as they each walked across the stage. I caught him wiping away a few tears as Kevin took his diploma. Mallory bowed as she shook hands with their principal, a tall, stern looking woman who rolled her eyes as Mallory stepped to the side and made a silly face at her parents' cameras. Ryan smiled at me as I took his picture, his hands fidgeting with his diploma.

Kevin leaned back in his seat, Mallory taking a sip of her milkshake next to him. "I thought I would feel different somehow, like more adult or something."

"Yeah," Mallory said. "It just feels like another summer break."

"Maybe it'll come later, when we're not going back to West Haverty in the fall."

"I mean, it's not like we're done with school or anything." I replied.

We finished eating and drove back to Kevin's apartment. He picked up the mail from their slot as we went up the stairs. Jeremy was there when we got inside, working in his office down the hall. I could hear his keyboard clicking as we went into the kitchen. Mallory sat down in one of the chairs at the table as Kevin began looking through the mail. Ryan stood next to me as I looked at pictures that were stuck up on the refrigerator with magnets. There was one of Kevin and Jeremy from what looked like a Christmas several years ago. Kevin had a Santa hat on his head as he sat in front of the couch they still owned in a house I imagined was the one he had lived in before his parents died. Jeremy sat on the couch, a still-wrapped present in his lap. They both had big grins on their faces, and I imagined one of their parents was standing behind the camera, still alive and happy. Things had changed so much for them since that picture was taken.

Ryan slipped his arm around me and squeezed and I leaned my head against his.

"Holy crap . . ." Kevin said behind us, and we turned to see him holding a letter in his hands, staring down at it with wide eyes. His lips were parted slightly.

"What is it?" Mallory said, worry coming over her face quickly.

Kevin looked up at Ryan and me, then to Mallory. "I did it."

"Did what?" she asked.

"I got it. I got the freaking scholarship. I was one of the top scores on the test. I got it, you guys! I friggin' got it!"

A look of pure joy came over Kevin's face, his eyes brightening up as his mouth fell open in a massive smile. I could see his hands shaking, the letter still grasped between them.

Mallory stood up and went to his side, looking over his shoulder at the letter, her eyes moving back and forth over the page. Her mouth fell open.

"Oh my gosh! Kevin!" She turned and threw her arms around him as they both began laughing. She let go of him and Ryan and I quickly dove in for a hug as well. His arms wrapped around me tighter than they ever had before, and when we stepped back I could see tears at the corners of his eyes.

Mallory came up and placed a hand on each of his cheeks, looking into his eyes, "I knew you could do it. I'm so proud of you, Kevin."

"What's going on?"

We all turned at once to see Jeremy standing in the doorway. He looked at us all curiously, a pencil behind his ear, his shoulders tense like always.

Without saying a word, Kevin lifted his hand that held the letter out to Jeremy. Jeremy stepped forward, looking at Kevin as he took the letter from his hand. His eyes fell to the page and read. His expression didn't change as he looked up at Kevin.

"Is this real? Did you really get this?"

Kevin smiled at him, "I really got it, Jer. I really did it."

I watched all the muscles in Jeremy's face relax, his mouth falling open into a smile. "You did it? You got the scholarship?"

"I got the scholarship!"

"You got the motherfreakin' scholarship!" Jeremy's hands flew into the air, still holding on to the letter. "You did it, Kevin! You're going to a university!! You got it!"

He lunged forward, arms out, wrapping around Kevin in a bear hug. Jeremy practically lifted him off the ground as they laughed and shook each other. Without letting go of each other, they continued to speak, their voices rising.

"You did it!"

"I did it!"

"Of course you did it! You're a genius! You're smarter than all of them! Of course you got it!"

"I actually did it!"

They eventually stopped jumping and shaking and their voices got quiet, but they still hung on to each other, their arms never falling from each other's backs. Their heads rested on each other's shoulder as they stood in the middle of their tiny kitchen, eyes closed.

They had finally gotten a break. After all that time they spent work-ing so hard all the time, they finally got a moment to rest, to breathe. Happiness filled my entire body as I watched them cling to each other. They were all they had and they had made it work. I couldn't think of anyone who deserved to feel this moment of peace any more than they did. Kevin had done it. They both had done it. And now they got to rest and celebrate.

Jeremy slowly stepped back from Kevin. He lifted a hand to the back of Kevin's neck, holding it still as he leaned forward and gave him a small kiss on his forehead. Leaning back, he looked into his eyes.

"You did good, kid. You did *so* good."

Kevin nodded and patted Jeremy on the arm. Jeremy stepped back and rubbed a hand across his face.

"Let's order pizza tonight. It's a special occasion and I think we can spare $30 for that. You guys gotta stay for dinner. We're celebrating." He smiled at us before stepping out of the kitchen and back down the hall.

Mallory stepped forward and wrapped her arms around Kevin again, leaning her head against his chest. He rested his head against hers and closed his eyes.

"Are your friends coming over tonight?"

I turned from where I was kneeling on my bed to see my mom standing in the doorway. She was leaning against the doorframe watching me. Judging from her relaxed posture and the way her head was casually resting against the wall, she'd been there for a while.

"Yeah, they should be here in a few minutes."

"Oh."

I hopped down from the bed, reaching to the nightstand to turn down the Van Morrison song that was playing on my radio. I looked at her, "Everything okay?"

"Yeah, it's fine. I was just wondering. It was so quiet tonight." She paused. "What are you working on?"

I glanced up at the collage I'd been piecing together for the past hour, "I got my pictures developed today and wanted to do something with them. There were too many to get frames for all of them, so I figured I would try this."

I turned back and watched her eyes move over the pictures taped to the wall above my bed, pausing on different faces and memories. She smiled, pointing to one lower on the wall, "I love that one, the one of you and Ryan. When was that?"

I looked closer at the picture she was pointing at. It was the one Mallory had taken of Ryan and me at the carnival. We were sitting next to each other on top of the picnic table we'd eaten at, his face turned towards mine, smiling. His eyes were lit up from the carnival lights. He looked peaceful, content. Orange and purple lights glowed around our heads. The children running behind us were a blur. We were the only thing in focus. It was beautiful. He was beautiful.

I hadn't really looked at a lot of the pictures in detail when I had picked them up. After I'd come home, I'd laid them all out on the floor and poured over them. There were several that I'd forgotten about, like the one of Mallory at the mall when she'd found the dress she wore to prom. Then there were some that I hadn't taken or even been aware of. One, higher up on the wall, was of Kevin and me at The Empty Cup. I wasn't sure when it'd been taken, but I was pretty sure Ryan was behind it. My face was at the front of the photo, laughing. Kevin was just behind me, slightly out of focus, laughing too. We both looked so happy.

"It was that night we went to the carnival" I said, finally. "I like it too."

My mom glanced over the wall for a moment longer before turning to go. "I'll let you finish," she said, looking back towards me from the doorway. "Do you want me to fix anything for you guys?"

"I think we'll be okay. Thanks, though."

"Okay"

"Mom?"

"Yes, sweetie?" Her eyes looked into mine for the first time in what felt like forever. For months, our conversations had been held with tears and distant eyes. Now, for the first time in so long, she met me eye-to-eye. It felt like we were seeing each again after being away for a while. It wasn't just her eyes. Her shoulders were higher, hands gentle and weightless as they held onto the doorframe. She looked better than she had in months.

"Are you okay?"

She gave me another soft smile, "Yeah, I'm fine."

"No, I mean . . . are you happy? Like in your life, are you happy?"

She looked back at my wall. I tried to see which picture she was looking at, but she didn't appear to be staring at any one picture in particular. It was like she was looking at the whole group of them. Her smile widened a bit as her eyes met mine again.

"I am. I'm happy. I haven't been for a long time now, but I finally feel like I'm on my way back."

"Are you sure?"

"I'm sure."

I smiled at her for a moment before turning back to the pictures.

"You know that none of what I've been feeling is because of you, right? I know that I've been upset for a long time now, but I just want to make sure you know that you were a good thing in all of it. You helped me get back to where I needed to be."

"Really?"

"Of course. If you hadn't been here, I don't know what I would have done. I wish I could have been more present in your life these past few months, more aware. I just hope we can make this summer before you go away to school a really special one. Does that sound okay?"

I smiled, "It does. I'd really like that. So you're really okay?"

"I am, my sweet son, I really am."

She tapped her hand gently against the doorframe before heading down the hall. I listened to the sound of her footsteps against the stairs as I turned back to my wall of moments.

I reached down and turned the volume back up on my radio, a warm beat flowing out of the speakers. Looking up at my wall, I looked over all the memories of the past year, all the people in my life. So much had happened that year, some good and some bad, but as I looked up at that wall and those pictures, all I could see was the good. I saw the friends I'd made and the moments I'd shared with them. I saw the boy that I loved laying on a blanket in the grass. I saw my mother laughing at something my grandmother was saying, her mouth open in an incredible, joyous smile.

Without realizing it, my body began moving along to the music coming from the radio. I closed my eyes, letting it take me over and slide me around the room. My body moved and danced across the floor, feeling lighter than it had in months. I opened my eyes and saw a shadow moving across the wall. Turning, I saw my friends. Mallory and Kevin stood behind me, dancing carelessly, looking simultaneously goofy and wonderful. Mallory's hair flew around her face, Kevin's hands swinging around his body. I stepped over to them and we danced, turning and bumping and swinging our hands through the air. We didn't care how we looked, we just danced. Because it felt good.

I looked up and saw him watching me from the doorway. My boy. My extraordinary, beautiful boy. He leaned his head against the door-frame, watching as I danced through Mallory and Kevin and over to him. I leaned into him, my forehead pressed into his. His eyes looked into mine and I felt whole. I felt good. I reached down for his hands, lacing my fingers through his, feeling his skin against mine and remembering the night I watched him sleep and fell in love with every part of him. He was mine. I was his. He was everything. I lifted his hands up and pulled him forward, into our dance. He fell against me, and we held each other and bounced back and forth. A smile lit up his face and moved onto mine.

I looked at Mallory and Kevin, dancing together and yet separately. Maybe they were okay. Maybe they didn't need to be together to be happy. Maybe the greatest romance you can have when you're young is the one you have with your friends.

Life wouldn't always be easy. But, as I held the boy that I loved and danced with my friends, I knew something. There were moments, moments I had all my life, but never even noticed. Moments like this. They were moments where everything was good, everything was beautiful, and maybe these were the moments I had to hold on to. These were the moments that would help me live.

As I moved around the floor with my friends, I felt free. I felt my body fill up with breath and my mind become clear. I wanted them all to feel it with me, all the people in my life, everyone that had been hurt. I imagined them all there: Milo, Mrs. Stroud, Brooke, my father, my mom. I imagined them all there dancing, moving along with us, feeling this clear, feeling this freedom. Because even if life wasn't perfect, we had this to hang on to. We had these moments with friends, moments with the people we loved. We had moments like this one that would lift us up above the rubble and show us that everything was okay, that we were okay.

I had these people and I loved them.

This novel wouldn't be in your hands today without some of the incredible people in my life. I owe them a huge thank you for helping me get to this point.

My Parents – Thank you for always allowing me space to be myself. I wouldn't be where I am today without the love and (let's be honest) patience you've given me. I never heard "be more realistic" in our home when talking about my dreams and goals. You never told me I couldn't be exactly who I wanted to be. I'll never be able to thank you for that, but I'll keep trying. You've given me a great life.

Mema and Granddaddy – This novel is dedicated to you for a reason. You've taught me more than I'll ever be able to articulate or thank you for in words. I'm grateful for every day of my laugh because of you. Thank you for the love, the advice, and the lessons. I love you tremendously. I'm so honored to be your grandson.

Bennett – Being your brother is one of my favorite titles. I hope I make you proud.

Roddy and Mary Kay – I'm eternally grateful for your generosity and kindness. I truly wouldn't be where I am in my life without you. Like, TRULY. Thank you for making space in your home and your lives for me (and Jake).

My Teachers – Thank you to the teachers (Chris Rice, Laurie Lawlor, Marcia Brenner, Ann Hemenway, Elizabeth Yokas, Doug Whippo, Sam Park) at Columbia College Chicago who pushed me and helped me become a better writer. The lessons and feedback you gave me will stay with me forever. I wouldn't have been able to get this novel to where it is without you.

Karen McKinley – You've been with me since we had to write the first draft of our novels in 3 months (Remember THAT?) and I'm grateful every day for our friendship. You've helped me so much over the years as I wrote, edited, rewrote, edited again, rewrote some more, edited a dozen more times, whined, and submitted this story to publishers (even if that part didn't work out lol). I'm thankful to have you in my life, not just for your feedback and writing advice, but for your wonderful friendship and kind heart. You're one of the best and I hope you never forget that. (Let's get sushi soon!)

Amber Burnett – HONEYYYYY! Where do I even begin??? You've been my best friend since my life in Chicago began (we'll forget the few months pre-Columbia (pre-Amber – P.A.) where we didn't know each other) and I can't imagine my life without you. You've been my ride or die through bad classes, bad jobs, bad weather, and running out of gas in Iowa at 11pm on our drive to L.A. Then you designed the damn COVER OF THIS BOOK! I just can't EVEN! I love you to the ends of the earth and back, and plan to buy you a steak next time I see you. I love you.

Jake Kenneally – Last, but certainly not least, Jacob. You are my favorite part of life. Nothing makes me happier than waking up next to you every morning. You've literally been by my side since I began this journey back in 2013 and I don't know how you've had the patience to deal with me and this for over 8 years. Thank you for loving me through every iteration of this story, through all my whining about how hard finding an agent is, and through all my crazy. You are the definition of a good man and I'm so glad I get to be in your life. I love you.

Bonus Thanks: Lady Gaga. Because it's my novel and I can thank her if I damn well choose to.

William Grant holds a BA in Fiction Writing and Photography from Columbia College Chicago. He's had work published in *Hypertext Magazine* and *The Lab Review*. He currently lives in the Chicagoland area with his partner and their cat. This is his first novel.

Instagram: @willtg

Twitter: @buzzishere